i

Footsex
of the
Mind

By Ian M Pindar

"The hottest love has the coldest end"

Socrates

Cover and logo design by John Keane
j_f_keane@hotmail.com

Contact via:
www.ianmpindar.com

Follow on Twitter:
@thewritingIMP

Also by the same author

Hoofing It: 1 The Robert Knight Trilogy
Hoofed: 2 The Robert Knight Trilogy
50 Mistakes of the Fledgling Fiction Writer (non-fiction)

Out soon

The Space Between the Notes

Acknowledgments

To the person who told me *'her'* story first hand, on the understanding I kept her identity secret–you know who you are, much thanks.
Sally McKenzie for a critical eye and further suggestions.
Rose Gibson for proofing that turned to editing, and a differing opinion about a part of this book, but that's the subjective nature of literature! Amber Mitchell for last minute corrections, proofing, and advice.
John Keane (j_f_keane@hotmail.com) for the usual technical and graphic assistance.

Chapters

Chapter 1

Charlotte was never ever late. She was sat at the bar in Claridge's twenty minutes before hand. Today was different. It had been seventeen years since she had hurtled out of Felix's life and into another one. She was running the scenarios of the lunch date through her mind, like she had many times before. Now there would be immediacy, now there would be nowhere to hide. She had ordered a glass of champagne. The end of the bar seemed the best position to adopt, rather than a table or a booth, always gave a great vantage point to people watch, something she never tired of. It was quiet and she was watching the skilled way the young attractive male and female bar-staff were serving the opposite sex, an easy way to maximise your tips. She remembered it well: big smile, *'Hi, what can I get you?'* Like a cocktail–three-quarters warm service, one quarter sexy suggestiveness.

There was a couple in the corner she could see with more clarity now her eyes had become accustomed to the low level lighting. He was much older, but the body language said; rich, maybe Russian, Eastern European, definite, not from money; his eyes betrayed his past, even though they tried not to. She could see that–eyes that could turn cruel if cornered, eyes that would not flinch if they watched–. She almost laughed at her own internal film noir narration. The woman was new, not a wife or long term partner, she was trying too hard; she did not want to lose him. Not that he was complaining about the lavished attention, she was at least thirty years younger–money can have that effect. A younger couple in their early thirties sat at another table, professionals, British. She would have said they were teachers, but the holidays had not yet started. Just married, an anniversary, she guessed, waiting for a table in the Foyer Restaurant, just like her. Their first time here; excited by it, drinking it in, trying to remember the details to tell their friends; the type that would film their room, or take pictures of the food; then put it on their social media page–if they were even rooming here. She guessed maybe they were northern, down for a few days in a budget hotel, but this was their highlight. Excited that a celebrity Chef might be cooking for them–they should be so lucky, but one thing was certain, the one who put his name and smiling face to the menu would be out to puff his chest up and check bags for tomato ketchup, if he was.

She was about to analyse a lone older woman that shouted 'old money', maybe theatrical, content to flick through a glossy magazine, when a middle aged businessman entered at the far end from where she was sat. He scanned the room as he walked to the bar, looked past the couple sat in the middle and smiled towards Charlotte. He stopped before he reached the bar, as if repelled by a mild electro-static force. The female barmaid mirrored him on the other side, and he ignored her. He strode towards Charlotte, maintaining eye contact all the way; his smile now receding into a slight grin. She had no idea who he was. A few moments earlier he was a businessman off duty, the sort who had no concept how to dress once the conformity of the suit and tie were removed–dressed like a collection of adverts you get in the back of a Sunday supplement, the sort that made M&S look cutting edge.

'Hi, how are you?' He said as he placed his room key-card down in front of her. She noticed the tan around where his wedding ring would normally be.

Then she tried to evaluate the accent; North-North-American or Canadian; Chicago, Detroit, Toronto – he was a city boy. She did not answer him.

'Can I get you another drink?'

'No thank you. I am waiting for my husband.' It was a lie, but it was the quickest way to get rid of him without being rude. Horror flashed across his face, it ruddied and his body hardened with embarrassment.

'Oh gawd, I'm *so* sorry. I thought you were my... date. I am *so, so,* sorry.' She warmed to his genuine penitence and could not help thinking; *you might need that for your wife one day.*

'Don't worry–just a mix up. I've had an argument with my husband and I have brought him here to apologise.'

'I'm so sorry to have bothered you. I will get out of your face.'

She did not want to be talking to him when Felix arrived. It would be ridiculous trying to explain what was happening. He scuttled off down the opposite end of the bar, ordered a beer and sat at a table with a paper, out of her view. Charlotte sipped her champagne, smiled and re-composed herself. She was scanning the wine list when she saw Felix appear in the doorway. She broke into a spontaneous smile and he waved across to her. He looked good, dressed smartly in a grey suit with narrow lapels, the height of fashion at the moment and it took a good few years off him; a crisp white shirt, polished black shoes. Still had all his thick black hair, with a hint of salt and pepper around the side-burns. Clean shaven, the gait and confidence of a Bond lead, with the sort of face that only gets better looking with age. She lifted herself away from her stool and they smiled and kissed each other on the side of their cheeks. Pulling away, they were both uncertain if they should do the French double-kiss. Instead, they considered each other, and Felix stepped back from her to get a full-length perspective.

'You're looking fantastic! You've really looked after yourself.'

He pulled away a little further, and eyed her up and down. The years had been very kind to her – to both of them. She had put on about seven pounds, and Felix maybe twice as much, but he could afford to. She was wearing a black shoulderless cocktail dress. White pearls hung down from her neck and matched the bracelet on her left wrist. The dress stopped above the knee and she had a pair of black tights on, maybe stockings. Her black velvet stilettos made them both the same height. He searched her face for wrinkles, but found none. Her hair hung over her shoulders in a light wave, shimmied when she did, coloured two tones of blonde.

Charlotte blushed, *'Rubbish…* Not as good as *you.* You look great.'

'I was worried you might have ballooned.'

'Not as worried as I was about you.'

She spluttered a giggle at him.

'You look *stunning!*', a flirty glint in his eye.

'Stop it.'

'Come on let's sit down,' patting the bar stool beside him at the same time.

They both perched on their stools facing each other across the corner of the bar. Felix continued, 'You *do* look very good, very attractive… the years have been incredibly kind.'

'Please stop, you charmer. You're embarrassing me.'

'You really have looked after yourself *very well.'*

'You have to; the middle classes are not allowed to be fat.'

'It's great to see you again. I was just thinking about the last time I saw you– two years after we finished college, at the Alumni's reunion, fifteen years ago?'

'Yeah, fifteen years ago, seventeen since we finished… *College I mean*?'
Felix threw Charlotte an acknowledging look and tightened his lips in recognition.

'I know what you meant Charlie.'

'Why do you think I have asked you here, Felix?'

He stopped and thought about it again, like he had for the last five days since she had e-mailed him; then with more focus after their brief chat on the phone. It felt strange to be hearing her voice after so long; a diminishing echo from the past. After the initial awkwardness, when they were deciding where to meet. It was a bit like old times; when they were going out at University. He had come to the same conclusion every time. He'd told Trist he was meeting her, and Trist had said something strange, *"good."* Which *was* strange because initially, all those years ago when they first split, Trist said he was not getting involved, and that he was not getting caught in the middle, having to make a choice over loyalty. As the years had passed he never reported on Charlotte, and Felix never asked.

'Forgiveness, you want my forgiveness?'
Charlotte looked at her empty wine glass and twisted it in her fingers, then back up at Felix.

'I suppose, ultimately I do, really.'

He let her dangle–it had taken a long time to get over Charlotte, at least two brief relationships, and he had done what a lot of people do; thrown himself

5

into another relationship, thinking it would wash away the memory of Charlotte, but it had not. He had told himself as they were both Americans, it was a cultural thing, but he knew deep down that was not true. They were both great women, but he was just not ready, and he had just not moved on from *her*. He could not help feeling mild anger now he was face to face with her after so long. They were so happy then, and she had discarded him, discarded rather than finished with him. Felix had seen a Tennessee Williams play a long time ago. He forgot the name of it now, and in the play, a character used the expression, *'you quit me,'* and that's what she had done; she had *'quit'* him. No one had been lined up–that's what he couldn't fathom. He could understand if she thought she had a better offer, even if he did not agree with it–how could he? She had no one. That was odd. His mother had told him he had put off the grieving, because that was what the break-up of a long term relationship was like. It was like a death. She also had a theory about the length of the relationship and how long it takes to get over it. He forgot all the details now, but she had been right in his case. He had not eaten for a whole week, and much of the second, it was like he was on hunger strike. Charlotte had refused to talk to him. She had left college the week before. Her mum had come to collect her things when her dad was at work. When the car was packed, Charlotte said she wanted to go with him to the garden in the grounds. The gardens were in bloom and meticulous. She found a secluded private bench and the words that followed haunted him for years.

"This is the hardest decision of my life, Fe." She held both his hands in hers as she said it. "I have to finish with you, because I cannot make you happy, and you deserve to be happy." She had started to cry, hysteric.

6

She shook her head from side to side, slow to start with, tried to wrestle more words out, gagged and paralysed by her own self-flagellation. Felix looked at her transfixed; *disbelief* was too weak an adjective for what he felt. He thought she was going to say they should get married sooner rather than later, thinking that was why they had come somewhere so quiet, so magnificent, away from the buildings, away from the people, somewhere clandestine to make the occasion more special–*theirs*. He managed to wrestle a few words out: *"No, no…"* , then something more lucid: "You have used me, used me for the last two years Charlie." She couldn't speak; raw emotion held her captive. She composed herself *just* enough. "I haven't, *honestly*. You have to believe me. *I haven't*. I cannot make you happy Felix, not forever. You deserve to be happy. Someone as beautiful as you deserves to be happy." He was too stunned for logical words; he was good with words, but not now. She had left it until the very last possible moment.

They had made love that very morning, as soon as he woke up. They had made love for two reasons; firstly, they would not see each other for over a month, as Charlotte was going to South America, and secondly, and *much* more important, because they *loved each other*. You can only make love to someone if you *love* them.

Charlotte had held Felix's head in her hands, staring deep within him, swimming inside his head. He thought she was going to commit herself to him for the rest of their lives; he felt her love for him was all consuming, the real thing. The search was over even before he realised it had begun. He was so confused, so horrified, grief-stricken that he could not speak. He could not make any sense of it. They had been so close, so inseparable for the last two years. He knew there was no one else, no cuckoldry, no head-turner, no ex. *"No…"* Felix shouted while shaking his head from side to side in her arms, not trying to break free, she tried to steady him. *"Why?"* He repeated several times and Charlotte replied with the same reason. "It's not you, *it's me*. I cannot make you happy long term. I know I will hurt you much more down the line." Charlotte had got up to leave and Felix had grabbed her wrist. "There has to be something else Charlie. *What is it?"* He implored her to tell him. "It's just me… There is no one else." He chased after her; implored her further not to abandon him. Her mother was stood by the estate car, ready to take her on the next part of her journey, away from Lady Margaret's, away from him. He chased her towards the car, as she quickened, he grabbed at her arm to stop her, to stop *this madness, her madness.* Charlotte spun around at the side of the passenger door; her eyes red and translucent from the sobbing tears. He was still too stunned to comprehend the full extent of what was happening. "Don't go, stay here, we can sort this out. *Don't go… Please don't leave me. Please."*

"I have to go." He looked past her at her mother; he thought it strange she was not upset that her only off-spring was so distraught.

"I will come with you. We will sort it out at your parent's."

"I have to go, I am *so, so, sorry. I did love you, Fe.*"

"DID?"

''*Still do*, you know that."

"Then stop this madness now Charlie." He shouted at her, stern, "I want to spend the rest of my life with you." A few of the students were trying not to rubber-neck them, but they were difficult to ignore; still

8

her mother said nothing. Charlotte half turned to get in the car and Felix grabbed her tighter.

      "I won't let you go Charlie."

      "I'm so sorry." She was crying more.

      "No, I will not allow it."

Without speaking her mother got in the driver's seat and started the engine. Charlotte trapped him in her gaze. How could she have done this to him? How could he have done this to her? How could they have done this to each other?

      "I have to let you go Felix. It will be for the best. I know it does not feel like it now, but I cannot make you happy. You will see, it will all be ok for you."

He let her slip from his grip and slide into the seat. It was a scene he would replay; beat himself up about for a long time afterwards. He let her shut the door on him, and allowed her to be driven away with tears cascading from her face. Helplessly, he watched the car slip out of view from the walled car park onto the road, and drive south to her parent's house. He was letting her slip out of his life. He was allowing her to punish herself as well as him. It was when the first shadow of realisation started to cast itself over the very edge of denial. His body vibrated, with the realised horror, the rest of their happy-ever-after lives together extinguished and evaporating away for no rational reason. It was then the grieving started, crashed over him, the pain that would rage and wash for months, and then only subside over the next few years. He fell to his knees like a pierced Roman Emperor. Instead of reaching to the heavens for a last soliloquy to his guilty perpetrators, his head fell into his hands, his body sagged and he sobbed, abandoned sobbing. His pain radiated out for all to see, almost tangible like the concentric ripples of a pond, human suffering that cannot be left alone. Trist appeared at

9

Felix's side and knelt beside him, cushioned and gathered him in to his chest, guided by his arms. He was a helpless toddler again. It had been years since he had felt this slain, even with Trist's reassuring touch.

"What is it Felix?"

Trist moved to the front of him and Felix fell into his shoulder, listless, arms and palms wrapped around him were no reassurance. Trist waited for him to burn himself out a little and coaxed him away from him, so he could see his raw face, before he got his second wind. Felix spoke though mucus, voice tremulous.

"Did you know?" He accused, while searching and condemning with stabbing eyes.

"I don't know what has happened Felix, honest. *What is it?"*

"She has left me!" Trist tried not to cry as he saw his joint best friend so bereft, so forlorn for the first time. Then there came the word that Felix would remember for the rest of his life–not the word; he already knew the word, the way Trist uttered it. It was the word that told him Trist could not disguise his anger towards Charlie, when maybe he should have been neutral in such matters between his two closest college friends, the word that reassured Felix that Trist had no idea.

"Fuck!..." Followed by, *"The stupid FUCKING BITCH!"*

Felix left the past behind and returned to the present. He did not like the discomfort of that moment, a moment that stretched for far too long afterwards. There was no duplicity between fact and fiction, no clouding of memory. Now he was in control–the choice between revenge or forgiveness.

10

'Let's see what words of redemption you can conjure up.'

'Am I on trial Felix?'

'Do you feel as though you're on trial?'

'A little, *yes*.'

Felix smiled at her. He was not a vindictive person, but he was judge, jury and executioner. He could never bring himself to torture her; never in the way she had tortured him, at least; that's what he told himself.

'Not a trial by jury of your peers Charlie.'

'Should I be more worried or less?'

'Do you believe in the Magna Carta?'

'From what I can remember, yes.'

'Then definitely far more worried. But the good news is they have not killed a witch in Britain since 1727!'

Charlotte twisted in her seat a little, and half smiled and half frowned. This is not how she had imagined the opening gambit between them, after the 'Hello, how are you?'

'Don't be horrible to me Felix,' she pleaded.

'Sorry... You can't technically be a witch, as witchcraft was removed from the statute books in 1947.'

She pleaded further.

'Stop it Fe! Don't be horrible. It's not in your nature.'

'Sorry. I will stop.'

'You have every right. But you're better than that Fe.'

'I will stop. I'm sorry– out of order.'

The *'sorry'* took them back to that last day together at college. Charlotte gestured over to the bar staff and ordered two glasses of champagne without asking Felix what he wanted.

'Are you going to forgive Felix, or are you going to exact your revenge?'

'I *may* forgive you, whether God will forgive you, *that's* another matter.'

They both laughed at the thought together.

'God doesn't want me. The Devil would be in two minds?'

'Is it that important that I forgive you for something that happened seventeen years ago?'

She gave him an intense stare; he had seen the look many times before. It was a look that said *I am being serious now. I want you to believe what I am telling you.*

'Yes it's important to me. I was horrid to you.'

Felix thought about challenging the word, '*horrid*,' when the champagne arrived. Charlotte passed a flute to Felix.

'*A toast.*'

'To what?'

'To all the good times, only the good times, that no one can take away.'

'Ok,' agreed Felix, and he proposed, more succinct, '*To the good times.*' Charlotte echoed his sentiments, as their words over-lapped.

'There were so many good times Fe.'

'Could have been a lot more though Charlie?'

Charlie thought about the most tactful response.

'Maybe, let's not dwell on the negative, life's too short.'

Felix was about to speak. Charlotte reached across and put her index finger near his lips, held it there and smiled.

'Nothing negative, accentuate the positive. *Yes?*'

The finger transported him back to the disabled toilet in the *Jules Verne* restaurant on the first stage of the Eiffel Tower, when she'd dragged him in there. At least that's how he remembered it, and before he could protest. She had put her finger over his mouth and the clumsy release of the button on the waistband of his jeans. It was the first thing he always thought of when he pictured or saw the Eiffel Tower. He remembered years later taking his children up, and it was still all he could think about, Charlotte and him in the toilet together, young lovers, disregarding the world. He had exchanged a few uncharacteristic cross words with his wife, when their daughter wanted to use the same toilets, and he did not want to take her in, even if it was not the exact the same cubicle; it was in the same place, the same ghosts might be there. It was a place that brought back so many memories of what might have been. What if he and Charlotte had stayed together? It might have been be their child they were taking to the toilet. It would have been them exchanging knowing glances, both of them smiling and giggling at how their love raged, and how they thought it could never ever be extinguished. It may have been them having a romantic break, and just for old time's sake…?'

'Ok, I will behave. I promise.'
'Shall we go and eat?'
'Why not.'
They walked the short distance to the Foyer Restaurant; most of the tables were full. The Maître d' caught Charlotte's attention from the opposite side of the room near the main entrance and wandered over smiling.

'Your table is ready, if you would like to follow me, *Madam, Sir.*' They followed him to the opposite

13

corner of the room and were seated at a small table. It reminded Felix of a spy meeting in a film. 'I will have your wine brought over, Madam.'

'How did he know what wine you wanted?'
Charlotte laughed before she spoke.

'He had it flown in this morning.'
Felix fired an obtuse look at her; not quite sure if she was being serious or not.

'I can't get too pissed. I have to be at the 'House of Common People' for four.'

'Sorry I took it upon myself to order some wine. I was here fifteen minutes before you. What are you doing at the house of parlez?'

'I have an interview with the Deputy Prime Minister.'

'Anything exciting?'

'I wouldn't have thought so, *would you?*'

'I don't know, I've not really kept up with recent events that much.'

'Lucky you then.'

'Will you be asking him about his secretary?'

'I could ask. He wouldn't answer though.'
A sommelier brought a free standing silvered wine cooler over to the side of the table; condensation clung to the side in droplets. They both stopped talking and watched a little intrigued as he pulled the green bottle from the iced water and dried it with a crisp white towel. All three of them turned their attentions to the twisting of the corkscrew. When it *wacked* out of the neck he proffered it towards Felix, by hovering it over the tall glass in front of him.

'Would you like to try it, Sir?'

'The Mademoiselle is the expert.' He pointed towards Charlotte with an open hand.

'Please, excuse me.'

14

After he had poured a soupcon into her glass, Charlotte brought the glass to her nose with assured elegance and smelt it.

'Yes, fine thank you.' They watched the smart dressed waiter fill their glasses with an elegant final twist of his wrist and small kink of his neck. 'You can take the red wine glasses. We will not be requiring those, thank you.'

Felix was impressed with the confident way Charlotte had sniffed the wine to ascertain whether it was off or not. He would not risk that, would have to have a quick taste to double check, save the embarrassment if it was corked. He could not recall the last time he had tasted wine that was 'off.' Felix nodded at her, as the wine waiter departed.

Felix pulled the wine from the cooler, careful to capture any stray drips falling onto the white heavy linen tablecloth with his own napkin. He read the label on the front and was surprised not to find a label on the back. *Henri Bourgeois Sancerre Etienne Henri*, he read in his head.

'It's one of my favourites.'

'You didn't really have it flown in did you?'

Charlotte liked the fact he thought she had. She joked further about the quality of the wine being substandard in such a high end hotel. She refused to tell him how much she paid for it, even though he asked, he could not help himself. Charlotte admonished him for even asking, and then giggled. She informed him the wine had not come from the hotel but from Harrods down the road–probably in a white van. The wine momentarily lost part of its glamour, before both of them dismissed the image. She added for further clarity, at the risk of sounding repetitive, that she was paying for everything.

'Should I protest?'

15

'Waste of everyone's time.

'You were starting to tell me about Politics.'

'Oh you haven't missed much. All the parties start to merge into one after a while. It used to be exciting–now they just fight over the middle ground, and all wear the same suits. Labour do it because they think they look smart and that's what the electorate want: the Tories do it because they don't want to remind the plebs how rich they really are. They all use the same hand gestures, and you're not always sure which party they are in until the caption comes up. Can you imagine how dull *Spitting image* would be now? It makes a refreshing change to meet an extremist. Anyway, let's not talk about politics it's *incredibly tedious.'*

Charlotte drained her glass. 'Do you want some more champagne, Fe?'

'White wine and champagne, you're pushing the boat out aren't you pet? I can't get too pissed.'

Charlotte laughed, then carried on giggling, 'I love it when you say *pet*; it's so funny, and so, you know?'

'Eeye, I know Pet!'

She laughed again louder. The people at the next table smiled at her, thinking she was merry, which she was now. She did not often drink at lunch times.

'Talking of politics, how are your mum and dad, is he still lecturing up in Newcastle? Is your mum still working?' Are they well, *Felix, pet?'*

Felix nodded to acknowledge her mimicry.

'Eeye canny like, eye smashin', ney problems.'

'You can stop the colloquialism now if you want, but I like it, always have.'

'Not always if I remember rightly.'

'I was pissed and young and bit up my own you know what.'

'You'll find it's your *arse, pet.'*

16

'Don't embarrass me Felix. I was wet behind the ears– thought I was, you know?'

'Better than most people?'

'Don't Fe, I was young, a little effete. *It was* a long time ago… Be nice to me, *please*.'

Felix filled Charlotte in about his family. His dad was still lecturing in Psychology up in Newcastle– even though he had been offered a promotion at Edinburgh, they had decided not to take it; their roots were too strong in the area. His mother now only worked three days in her psychoanalysis practice, after a scare with breast cancer five years previous. When Felix had told her that his mother was undertaking more and more *cognitive behaviour therapy* work; Charlotte had said something that Felix had found quite interesting:

'*Cognitive behaviour therapy*, Freud would not approve.'

He thought about picking her up on her Freud comment, but passed over it, instead; reminded Charlotte they still had the same place in France. Charlotte remembered it well. She had only been the once, but adored it. She smiled at the thought of her arriving there and the state she was in; made a mental note to herself to mention it later, as not to interrupt Felix in full flow with his life-time after her and his potted family history. She thought of *BC* standing for: *Before Charlotte*, then thought AD could be: *After Degrees* or *After Devastation.* She missed the full details about his brother because of this. His brother, now married for twelve years, something about law and barristers and a child, maybe a girl, Flora or Laura? *Married for twelve years*; when she last knew him he did not even have a girlfriend. The end of their love affair seemed even longer away now, even though he was flashing through the proceeding fifteen

17

years. Felix protested that he was talking too much and it was all about him. Charlotte countered and begged him to continue, with reassuring words of encouragement. She loved listening to Felix. When they had first met, in the rage of love, Felix had read Charlotte bedtime stories: The *Arabian Nights* and *Aesop's Fables*. She had thought at the time there is no better way to fall asleep: make love, be read to like a child–while the protective searchlight of love shone down on her, then wake up and make love again in the morning if time allowed: time always allowed back at Lady Margaret's. She remembered the old second hand copy of *Aesop's Fables* he bought her as a Christmas present and the message at the front: 'And the moral of the story is... I love you. Felixxx.' She remembered the tears falling down her face; then her father's when he read it after her.

'Enough of my family, what about yours?'

'Mum is mum, and dad started his own investment firm about ten years ago and two years later he had a heart attack.'

Felix was shocked, '*Shit*, I didn't know.'

'Survived it... but then two years later he had an even bigger one and died on the spot–'

'*Oh shit*, I am really, really, sorry.'

'He worked too hard, threw himself into his stressful work, and it was even more stressful for him without me there... and then put my mum in the mix.'

'I'm really sorry to hear that Charlie, will you make sure you pass on my condolences to your mum... *promise?*'

'Of course, my dad loved you... He was really upset when we, you know...'

'Yeah. I loved him, he was fantastic your dad, great guy, so genuine.'

'I miss him Fe, even now, *more now*. It's supposed to get easier?' Charlotte started to well up.

'Are you ok? I don't know how I'd react if one of my parents died?'

'No, I'm fine, you're such a compassionate man, always in tune.'

'Not sure about that, but are you sure you're ok?'

'Yes, yes, thanks for asking though.'

'What about your mum, how is she now?'

'I think she was very upset, but they never spent that much time together anyway, and at least she does not have to worry about money.'

'Your mum is a bit more complex.'

'You're always so tactful, clever with words, she liked you, *yes she really did*, well, as far as my mum can come to liking anyone that is.'

'Is she well?'

'Physically, yes; let's not talk about my mum, let's have a toast?' Charlotte had started on the Sancerre, even though Felix had not quite finished his champagne.

'To what?'

'To friendship, and...'

She trailed off, they clinked their flutes together and repeated the phrase.

'To friendship.'

'Even when one person has been a bit of a you-know-what?' Charlotte said.

'Let's wait for the verdict, later.'

'Ok, yes. I assume you are the foreman?'

'You assume correctly.'

'Have you seen any of the old crowd recently?'

She informed him that she had lost touch with most of them a long time ago. She had seen Margot about five years ago in Australia. Her husband was an executive in a big mining company and she was still based up in Darwin with her kids, bored out of her mind. She had filled Charlotte in with as much information that she had on the old crowd from Lady M's, and Trist had as well. She kept in contact with Margot through Facebook still. 'Looks after her kids and doing some part-time History teaching,' she elaborated further on Margot when Felix asked her for more details. Charlotte concluded by saying:

'Nearly everyone is ploughing their intended furrows as far as I can see.'

'Do we all have intended furrows?'

Charlotte sipped on her wine. Felix could see she was cogitating, giving her riposte some deeper analysis.

'Most people, yes– little boxes made of ticky tacky and all that. You're one of the exceptions; you should have done something more conventional I suppose, like politics, law, civil service, but you have a much more exciting life because you didn't.'

'It might look exciting, but I spend most of the week staring at a computer screen trying to think of something incisive and witty to write.'

'And you always seem to manage it from what I've seen.'

'Not sure about that, nearly always manage some copy, the good thing about my column is you can always write less and no one notices.'

'Your body of work is amazing; you seem to do it so effortlessly.'

'It's not effortless, I can assure you. It's lots of research and even more hours of writing, re-writing and editing.'

'At least you love your work, and you are not sat behind a desk watching the clock.'

'Yeah, there are much worse ways to earn a crust.'

'Giles has done very well for himself with his writing.'

'*The thinking man's thinking man* is what The Spectator called him!'

'Pass the sick bag.'

The waiter walked over. Felix felt the staff here always looked as though they had been dressed by their mothers, and were going for an interview for a job they really wanted, but were not the best candidates. He found the atmosphere of supposed relaxed formality was more like ostentatious servitude. 'Are you ready to order Mademoiselle, Monsieur, or do you need a few more minutes?'

'A few moments longer, thanks.'

Felix retorted and opened his menu for the first time and scanned it without concentrating on anything in particular.

'What you having Charlie girl?'

Charlie smiled with tightened lips and her head wilted a touch off centre at the same time as she sipped her wine.

'I am having a small Caesar salad and then the sea bass… *and yes*, I'm paying; it's my treat.'

'*No, no*, we will go Dutch, like that time in Amsterdam.'

She laughed at him and the thought of that long weekend. It still made her laugh, the thought of when he pretended to be a Dutch Tour Guide. Taking a small group of American tourists through a part of the modern art museum, completely making things up, even the names of the artists and ridiculous stories about their lives:

"The artist normally took one photograph of his work, then he destroyed it. He refused to destroy the work he thought was sub-standard as a reminder to him and the world of imperfection."

"This artist was a cross-dresser, and was convicted of cruelty to dogs, even before animal rights existed. He must have been very cruel indeed."

"When this artist met Jean Miro in Barcelona they were arrested for fist fighting in the street, an argument about olive oil apparently. No one knows the full details."

"This artist said anything that is placed within a museum *itself* becomes a museum."

–Why would they not believe him?

She left their 'Holland' of nearly two decades passed.

'Enough, I insist, it's part of my apology.'

'Ok, no point in having an argument about it, not with the price that Sancerre is going to cost?'

'Life is too short to drink cheap wine.'

'There is no such thing as cheap wine in here.'

'Good, what you having?'

'I will have,' he scanned the menu again. 'I will have the Rabbit terrine and the Tuna.'

'Do you want more champagne?'

'God no, this has gone to my head already.'

'What about the rest of the gang?' asked Charlotte.

'I went to a ten year reunion, and a lot of people turned up. I found it bit depressing.'

'In what way?'

'Well, I thought Oxford was going to be, you know, bohemian and radical, full of free thinkers and agent provocateurs, but it was quite boring. People that just wanted to get their heads down and work hard, preserve the status quo.'

'Welcome to the conservative public school system and not rocking the boat, *pet.*'

'Not stick their heads above the parapet, quite dull people and that shocked me, but then at this reunion they talked about Lady Margaret's like they had had such a wild and interesting time, do you know what I mean?'

'Oh I know what you mean, I was there, but everything is relative, for a lot of them after the constraints of private school, that was them letting their hair down.'

'And I got the feeling that people had only turned up to spy on how well or averagely other people were doing, just to make themselves feel better about their lives, not many seemed genuinely pleased about other peoples' successes, a sort of professional jealousy. Does that make sense?'

'Course it does, that's what they were doing. That's why I never go; most of those people were not that bothered about you while you were there–why the interest now?'

'Maybe, yeah, that's obviously a massive stereotype. What made me laugh was the first question was always: 'So what are you doing now?' From people that didn't even know who you were, not, *'How you doing?' 'Are you well?' 'Are you happy?'* It felt a bit false. I got the feeling that quite a few were hoping for more schadenfreude.'

'So like a school reunion?'

'But worse, without the warmth, and less shared bond–not the same teachers to discuss, or the bond of adolescence and the brotherhood of the local community.'

'Curtain-twitchers without the discretion.'
Felix laughed at her observation.

'I suppose so… A few people asked after you, not knowing we had split up ten years previous.'

'Oh, sorry about that.'

23

He ignored her apology.

'I think for most of them, we were defined by each other, a constant, and they thought we would still be together. We were like Bonnie and Clyde compared to most of them.'

Charlotte took a swig of her wine. The same waiter that had brought the wine came over.

'Are you ready to order now Mademoiselle?'

They ordered their food and Felix added he would like some 'sparkly water as well, thanks.'

Once the waiter had gone, Charlie laughed at him, *'Sparkly water.'*

'I only normally drink melted glacier water, but I know they don't have it here anymore.'

'And the others?'

They rattled through as many of the students as they could still remember, starting with the most important and obvious one, "Trist, as we both know was still a raving homosexual; great that he made silk; great that he has David as well." They agreed and could never have envisaged a few years ago that he would ever have settled down. There was a debate about whether he was settled, as he still had the predatory eyes for trade and there were sporadic outbreaks of bohemia in his life—Bohemia that Felix envied; but could not face; not these days. They laughed at the time Trist had declared himself: *bisexual, "I am now an equal opportunities fornicator, to comply with European law; no one will be turned away; unless obviously, they are minging."* They laughed further when they remembered the girl from the nightclub he'd brought back. *"When she got it out, I had to wave the white flag; I couldn't even look at it, never mind you know… I am now officially a homosexual again. I do not wish to comply with European law. I have left the hetro-European Union."*

They recalled his anguished face, and when they had pushed him, with reluctance he uttered the word through grated teeth, *"Vagina... I am no longer in the vagina business."*

'That's what I thought Oxford would be, like the last days of Rome, Caligula Fridays or ancient Athens, with people walking about like Plato, Socrates, and that bunch, discussing old theories and having loads of their own.'

'At least you had your own theories, most of them were *crazy*, but at least they were your own. You had the imagination to think some up and challenge the lecturers. They loved that.'

'The innocence of youth.'

Felix moved onto the *Tory Boys;* the *'Bully Boys' – 'The Three stooges,'* Charlotte called them; she could not remember all their names now: Cameron and Marcus were both Tory MPs in safe seats. William C had stepped down at the last election when his dad died, to become the Lord of the Manor. They both agreed that they liked William C, but the other two were slimy. Charlotte was dismayed that there was a chance that Marcus might get one of the big jobs and from there anything was possible.

'Can you image it, Marcus running the bloody country?'

'I'd rather not– he's upset quite a few in the present regime, but faces change and the old school tie, even if it's only Wellington, helps. The Hill Boys and Elitons don't like him, plays too much to the right of the party. Sorry I'm boring you wi–'

'Not at all, it's great to find out what people are up to.'

'I see on the web-site you have made The Lady Margaret's alumnis' role of honour.'

'That's not saying much is it? Nigella Lawson is on, and the ex-secretary of state for Education, the one that was a cross between Bertie Wooster and Dr Strangelove, who used to make up policy over breakfast like Alan Partridge.'

'I'm not on.'

'No big deal, your life will go on regardless, and anyway, it's best not to be on. Their finance office is always asking for donations if they think you have money.'

'Are you happy Felix?'

There was a change in tone from Charlotte, and she fixed him with a more intense stare. He knew the stare, it was a stare that did away with irreverence and required a serious grown-up answer.

'Wow, where did that come from?'

'Well, are you?'

'Depends how you quantify it? If happiness the absence of depression and misery, then of course I am, the edges between contentment and happiness, that's more blurred I suppose. Things change as we hurtle towards forty–'

'I'm not nearly forty, I'm mid-thirties…'

'We, plural,' He flicked his index finger and accused in equal measure. 'You were mid-thirties three years ago, unless you are delusional?'

Charlotte smiled at him and glugged on her wine at the same time. She did not like to dwell on growing older.

'Anyway,' She dismissed.

'You have a different perspective on life, your kids are the focus. You have to be less selfish, face up the fact you cannot party like you used to, however boring it seems; you settle down and try and get a good fit…'

'But, are you happy?'

26

'Yeah, course I am, I have never had the Churchillian black dog thing.'

'You have always been the type of person that would be happy, whatever you did, whoever you were with. People get pulled along with you and they become happy in your company.'

'Not sure about that?' He frowned as he said it.

'It's true, you're a bit of a lefty, but you don't judge easily. You always give everyone a chance, take them at face value, forgive them somewhat for their institutionalised prejudices and ingrained ideologies.'

'Not sure again. How about you, *are you happy?*'

She took a sip of her wine again. She thought for a while.

'I was just thinking last week when I booked the restaurant, about the best meal I have ever had, *ever,* what is the best meal you have ever had Felix?'

'That time in Montmartre, at the Little Chef. That was the best steak I ever had I think, when I stopped being a vegetarian, still unsure whether to eat meat again, but sometimes the first is always the best and everything after that can be a bit of a let-down, don't you think?'

'Sometimes, yes.' She knew it was a slight dig at her, but had no option than to let it ride, leave it unchallenged. She continued. 'Do you remember the two restaurants, *Petit Chef* and *Grand Chef* were next to each other, and I asked what the difference was in French, and the surly Parisian waiter said, *'one is bigger than the other!'* Charlotte spluttered a giggle out.

'I also remember that hidden restaurant we found from the guidebook, near the Pompidou, down that little dark side alley, where they did Crème Brulee

27

and lobster as a starter, which we both agreed could not possibly work. So, I ordered it to find out, and it was so good, I could have cried.' Felix recollected.

'Gai Moulin Bistro, that was the name of the restaurant.'

'You're making that up.'

Charlotte disregarded his accusation, ''Oh God that was *amazing*, wasn't it?'

'*Incredible*... I've had so many great meals, the problem is, it's like that saying *'when you've had chocolate, you don't want wafer.'* You start to expect great food all the time. So where was yours then?'

'I'm not sure you really answered the question. Anyway, I have eaten at many of the top restaurants of the world. I hope that does not sound too pompous?'

'It does, but carry on.' She giggled at him and he smiled back at her.

'The best meal I've had was in Paros that time with you, do you remember, when we hired the scooter and we found that lovely taverna in the old woman's garden next to the sea. As she was taking our order, her husband landed in a little boat; he shouted over what he'd caught, and she told us. Just the freshness of the food, the beauty of the simple delicious ingredients–how food should taste–a few minutes old. I've told people that story and they think I'm taking the piss, but it was, and I was in love, not just with you, with life. There were no boundaries. I had escaped home; there were no rules, limitless possibilities. Do you remember?'

'Course I remember. We had the prawns and sword fish, and ice-cold local Greek white wine. She ran around her allotment like a whirling Dervish and picked vegetables from the soil and twenty minutes later they were on our plates with the sea food. It was like an honour to see where the food had come from. The wine was cold and the sea shimmered, and…'

'*And what?*' She demanded.

'Oh you know…'

'It was just magical, wasn't it? That's the best holiday I have ever had, *ever*. When we left Piraeus on the ferry and sailed through the warm Mediterranean night, just the two of us, not quite sure of our destinations; like we were escaping to something better; fugitives; bounty hunters. The guy from Spain was playing his guitar, and the pretty fishing house away from the main town, and those few days on Antiparos next to the nudist beach, that was fantastic.'

'Has it got better with time, with the rose tinted spectacles of nostalgia?'

'I don't think so, no, it really was the best holiday ever for me, maybe not for you?'

'Yeah, it was pretty special…. But I burnt my bum on the nuddy beach!'

They both remembered when Charlotte had to rub after-sun into his backside, and he laughed and smarted with the pain.

'It was funny.'

'First and last appearance for my arse.'

'The options seemed so limitless then, as though nothing could stop us, like we could have travelled onwards forever and never stopped, never got bored, always be ecstatic. Am I making sense?'

'Oh course you are, it was great.'

'But all good things come to an end, I suppose?'

'It was a long time ago, but the important thing was it was great while it lasted and we have some warm happy memories.'

'Do you really hate me for what I did to you? Be honest with me?'

Felix took a gulp of his wine and fixed his gaze on it. He thought about airing on the side of diplomacy. He had hated her for months, but hatred had disappeared now. It was only the recollection of distant anger he was experiencing–hated his own hatred, the fact he had smouldered with it for far too long. He should have let the memory of their relationship evaporate away, but he hadn't been able to. He had been held captive by what they had: and what they could have had; and that resentment stalked him for too long afterwards. He knew that unconditional love involves suffering somewhere along the line, but he thought he could rise above that; he had read enough poetry at school, enough novels, some rom-coms, to have dominion over love, and when he couldn't negate its unwanted damaging after-effects, he was annoyed with himself for his weakness; but that annoyance always travelled back to Charlotte's door. That was a long time ago now.

'I was angry with you, and probably for a long while to follow, after the initial disbelief and denial. Of course, you cannot love someone and they decide they don't love you as much, and they have the...' he paused. 'Have the strength to walk away.' It was not the right expression; he was a little infuriated with himself for choosing it; but decided not to correct it.

'I did you a favour, you know that, not at the time. I broke your heart, and for that I am truly remorseful, but I couldn't have given you the happiness you deserved then–'

'Absolute Bollocks.'

'There was no other way out for me. I had to break your heart.'

'Why did you leave, you didn't have to. We would have made it?' Charlotte could sense the residual heartbreak returning, rough in his tone, filed away in his memory, never to be reopened, no need. She saw the pain she had inflicted on him in his rigid body and his bewildered gaze.

'I don't think we would, you wouldn't. I would have damaged you more. You didn't deserve that.'

She detected his voice quicken, as the spectre of their separation returned. She wondered if he noticed as she had.

'I thought it was forever. I thought I could throw a saddle on you and tame you, whisper in your ear and calm you. I thought I had tamed you enough for us to be happy forever. I couldn't understand why you punished yourself as well as me? It didn't make sense.'

Charlotte stood up and ran towards the toilet with her napkin in her hand, leaving Felix alone at the table as the food arrived.

Charlotte returned.

'I'm sorry about that, you may have forgiven me, but sometimes, you know...'

'Let's eat and talk afterwards.'

Chapter 2

Felix finished first and he sipped his wine and watched Charlotte pushing her salad around the plate. She placed her cutlery together and pushed her plate away from her even though there was still half of it left. She smiled at him.

'Some say you have to have your heart broken and break someone else's in return, to fully understand life.' Felix broke the silence.

'But I bet you have never broken anyone else's heart, have you? That's where some people differ?'

'You would have to ask other people that, not me?'

'I bet it would be a very long fruitless search?' Felix poured himself some sparkling water and sipped from it, Charlotte poured herself a third of a glass of Sancerre.

'At this last reunion, Principal Stewart was there. Remember the night we went skinny dipping, and a local woman walking her dog made a complaint to the college, so he said he had to investigate it.'

'Now that was a night. All Trist's fault, remember?'

'Trist and cocaine, if I remember rightly.'

'He was coming back from some debauchery somewhere and bumped into us coming back from, where had we been?'

'A crappy ball at St Hilda's.'

'Oh yeah, Hogwarts without the magic.'

'Next thing we know we are down by the river snorting cocaine off each other's backs, formal wear abandoned.'

'I don't think it was that that the old woman objected to, even if she did possibly see us. It was more Trist, *"shut up you silly old cow, can't they make love? it's a free Country."*

Charlotte remembered how cold the water was even though it had been red hot weather for over a week. After the initial 'ahhrs' and 'hoos,' the half-hearted swim. Their naked bodies had clung together for warmth. Their warm unprotected exposure had welded them as one, their goose-pimples fitted together like a jigsaw, and it was not long, egged on by the cocaine and Trist from the bank; that their tongues were dancing together, and then, they were making love against the support of the jetty, Trist a ghost. The soft oozing mud massaging their feet, lost in each other, lost in the drugs, *'making love.'* It was probably not how the passing dog-walker saw it?

'No, "*shut up you silly old bag, can't two beautiful people make love*," and…'
"'Don't forget to pick up your mongrel's dog shit!'" They both chorused together and laughed loudly, stopped and exchanged the same smiles.

'Or it could have been when he'd snorted cocaine off your naked back and asked in all seriousness, off his head, *"can I come on your back, Felix?"'*

'He really was a deviant wasn't he?'

'He was pleading with you, saying how gorgeous your form was.'

'Egged on by you agreeing with him, and telling me not to be a spoilsport.'

She laughed before she said it. 'Let me come on yer back you repressed northern monkey.'
Her laughter was uproarious and contagious, Felix joined her, several of the diners and waiters looked over towards them, they checked themselves.

'What did P Daddy Stewart say then?'

33

'He said, he thought the woman's accusations were a little ridiculous, but there had been an accusation of foul language against her. He said it was very unlikely, but he said if you wanted to go skinny dipping, why did you not go to the lake on the sports ground next door?'

'Did you say we didn't want to get caught with cocaine on College grounds?'

'*Funnily enough*, I left that bit out. I lied like the last time we spoke to him.'

They both smiled at each other and the memory of that far away night; a night that played in their minds like a clip from a favourite film; a night that hummed with hedonism and grandeur, not just for Charlotte and Felix, but Trist as well. A warm summer's night when they could not conceive of growing old; a night with no day to follow; a night where they celebrated life in all its indulgent splendour: sex, love, friendship, hope; the list was limitless.

'It was a good night. I really miss you and Trist bouncing off each other, *us,* all of us together like the old days… Maybe we should all go out–that would be great?'

'Maybe, but I have not passed sentence yet. You might still have to go to prison… or a public stoning.'

'Yes, Your Honour,' she replied trying not to smile. 'Maybe he could come to the hanging. He would quite like to put the wig on.'

'Trist and you were like brother and sister back at Lady M's. You used to go shopping together like a couple of Imelda Marcos's on speed. Remember, you used to get the train to London and stay in a cheap hotel, if you even went to bed.'

'I miss the three of us together.'

'When did you last see him?'

'It's been a while now.' She thought about it, and Felix surmised she was trying to figure it out. 'Maybe six months, but I'm back for a while, so there are no excuses this time. I'm not in a rush.'

'Who have we missed out from Lady Margaritas?'

They started to run through more of the old students. Katrina had become parliamentary under-secretary to Lord Lincoln. Felix clarified she was still a lesbian and had had a civil partnership to Erica, who was at Oxford at the same time as they were, but Charlotte could not recall her. Erica now worked for The Labour Party—love across the political divide—love conquers everything. Charlotte was intrigued that they had both had babies from the same father, via a turkey baster.

They remembered the Astrophysicist who always carried a Ninja Turtle called Galileo, who was now stuck on top of a mountain in Chile looking at the stars. Charlotte would not have won any prizes for guessing he was single. They both laughed at the woman from Arbroath, whose name eluded them. She always brought smoked fish back with her that absolutely stank every time the fridge was opened. Felix thought she was now a teacher in Scotland, 'better access to her beloved fish.' Andrew, who now worked at the History Museum, "getting paid very little, *but intellectually rich,*" he had informed Felix when he bumped into him quite recently. Then there was the guy with the ridiculous bushular beard from Devon, David, who was addicted to *World of Warcraft* and somehow hacked into the programme and made a fortune selling virtual reality characters to the Chinese and Koreans. Felix quite liked him, Charlotte found him a bit creepy, and dubbed him '*Odd-Bod'*.

'What a way to spend three of the best years of your life; it's mind boggling isn't it?'

'Whatever makes people happy. He was harmless. I think it was a comfort blanket for him, definitely on the spectrum, and he made friends through it.'

'*See,* there you go, seeing the best in everyone and everything.' It was one of the things that she had loved about him, not to start with, she found it naive—she would have judged people before they opened their mouths', before Felix. Felix always saw the best in people, always prepared to give people the benefit of the doubt—innocent until proven guilty.

'I remember the day I started at Lady Margaret's and I was quite nervous, thinking I would be the only student from a state school and there was this beautiful woman sat with a quite short exquisite embroidered floral dress on, white with intricate purple and blue flowers, with green stems and foliage, short on purpose, reading Anna Karenina *in French.*'

'*Stop it.*'

'I thought she would be out of my league. I thought everyone was going to be beautiful and be able to talk to each other in several languages, chat to each other in Latin and ancient Greek.'

She pictured her eighteen year old self—calculated, framed for those that would look, waiting for people to come to her; the pretentious book part of the introduction: beautiful and intelligent, but not available to all, only those she so chose. She could pick, or at least she thought she could, hoped she could. Looking back in some ways, it was a wasted year. With more time with Felix, things might have been different. She might have grown more contented; might not have had the wobble that turned into an earth-shattering rip. Maybe…?

36

"*All happy families are the same, all unhappy families are different.*' That's why I read it. I thought I might find some answers as well as improving my French, and yeah, to try and look suave and sophisticated.'

'Aristotle might have been more pretentious, and that is where it's stolen from.'

'Harry who?'

'You certainly attracted attention. You had all the boys queuing up.'

'Fiction imitating fact... I was such an idiot in that first year. I never ever finished it you know?'

'Who does? Tolstoy certainly struggled.'

Charlotte sat back against her chair and looked around the restaurant and Felix watched her, when their eyes met again they smiled at each other. She imagined them meeting for an anniversary meal. How many years would they have been married now, thirteen?, fourteen? Would they be happy? Just contented, or just going through the motions? Would they have children? Would they have had to hire a baby sitter, or would they have an au pair? Would they have split up by now, or be on second marriages? Futile *ifs* and *buts*, they were here now. She should at least be grateful for that.

'Remember the Eiffel tower? I was crazed that day. I was infected with something... must have been hormonal.'

They both laughed.

'You were obsessed?'

'God yes, I don't know why, but I had always wanted to have sex at the top of the Eiffel Tower and the toilet was a compromise. I think it was all the times I saw it when I was studying in school and the

37

phallicness of it... *Priapic Paris.* All the times my bored mind wondered in lessons and settled on sex.'

'A disabled toilet!'

'Neither of us were disabled that day, if my memory serves me well?'

'You were crazed, definitely.'

'I will never forget that woman's face.'

'Remember what you were shouting?'

'It's so embarrassing, thinking back.'

'*Baise moi, baise moi,* but you were shouting it so loudly.'

Charlotte flushed a little.

'Not so loud Fe... I was turned on, consider it a compliment.'

'*Baise moi.*'

'*Ssh*, Fe.'

They both laughed and Charlotte shook her head along with a coy smile. Unsuccessful in her admonishment of him.

'Her bloody face, and she winked and smiled at me and said: *"The walls are very thin for young lovers!"*'

They both laughed again and sipped their wine. It was the occasional madness of Charlotte that Felix loved so much about her back then. It was often her spontaneous nature; that lifted them above most couples; that separated them and made their love affair even more special. Being spontaneous is easy on the cusp of twenty: not so nearing the mid-point mark with two kids at home.

'I remember we skipped down by the banks of the Seine on the way to Notre Dame, singing songs. What was that song we didn't know the words to properly—that 'James' song?'

Felix started to sing in a light lilting voice. He sang the first verse and the chorus, '…… *think you're so pretty.'* He finished.

Charlotte shook her head in unison with her smiling.

'And you sang 'La vie en Rose' so bewitchingly… Oh you know how that melted me– beautiful intelligent girlfriend singing in perfect French.' Charlotte beamed at Felix.

'Lorsque vous me baise, ciel soupirs.'

'All the lines, not just that one.'

Charlotte sang, encouraged by Felix's singing and cajoled by alcohol.

'It took your kisses to reveal that I was wrong, and love is real. Hold me close and hold me fast. The magic that you cast… This is la vie en rose, for me.'

Felix had forgot the pain of the past for a moment, forgot what came after the bewitching singing in Paris, remembered only that time, that point in their history. He remembered the room in Pigalle around the corner from the Moulin Rouge. He remembered falling into the big comfy wrought iron bed with the woman opposite, making love with the woman he loved, the first woman he had ever loved; her falling asleep in his arms and both of them waking in them in the middle of the day–the night still ahead of them.

'Sing the rest.'

'When you press me to your heart. I'm in a world apart. A world where roses bloom. And when you speak, angels sing from up above.'

'Oh that song, it still… you know?'

She reached her hand across the table and rubbed the back of his, like a grandparent might do with an upset grandchild. She moved it away and added.

'Yeah, I know. And the guns shot above our heads.'

'Remember you tried to teach me the words in French, and I was like a five year old.'

'A five year old would have been better.'

'I really was appalling wasn't I?'

'Appalling for you, *yes*. We stopped at the Musée d'Orsay before we got to Notre Dame and you bought that print of the workers scraping the varnish off the floor of the apartment building, remember?'

'Still got it in my study, I think it's called The Floor Scrappers. I look at it sometimes and it reminds me how fortunate I am. However mentally drained I get, there is someone out there working harder and longer than me, and probably for a lot less money.'

'Gustav Caillebotte, Le plancher des racloirs, eighteen-seventy-five.' She said with assured certainty in her voice.

'You're making that up?'

She smiled at him and the fingers of her left hand played with her hair.

'Yes, maybe, it was something like that though.'

'What about that time at your mum and dad's, on the bedroom balcony?'

'Oh god that still makes me cringe now... on that occasion it *was* your fault, I was practically raped from behind?'

'Oh yeah, that would be about right, in your mind, at first maybe!'

'You were feeling me up through my thin summer dress and you know how excited I get. It was entrapment. Next minute you have my knickers on the floor and you are taking me very roughly from behind, it was then...'

They both cringed and laughed at the same time and pictured her mother's stunned, then horrified face as she looked up and saw them, caught in the act of sex,

40

rather than love making–two beasts in a field. If she had caught them in bed and it was tender love making, then she might have possibly felt guilty. The uncompromising position her daughter was adopting over the Juliet balcony shifted the guilt well away from the mother to the daughter, and then her boyfriend!

'Your mother's face when she walked around the back and caught us. I couldn't look her in the eye that weekend.'

'She was only jealous.'

'Do you think she ever told your dad?'

'Probably not, no.'

'At least she didn't bring it up. I thought about that when those pictures of Will and Kate got published. If it had been you and me back then, and we thought no one was looking, the photos would have been a lot more incriminating and interesting?'

They both giggled, and then smiled at each other.

'Does it not turn you on to think about that, and some of the other things we did?'

Felix thought for a few moments.

'I'm still man, flesh and bone. Course it does, why wouldn't it?'

'Oh I don't know, it was a while ago and memories fade, I suppose.'

'But there are some things you never forget.'

'Do you ever, you know?' She winced, a little embarrassed.

'What?'

'You know, ever?' She made an almost undetectable jerking movement near her abdomen with a tightened fist. Felix mimed the same and they both laughed.

'Nearer the time it was one for the bank...'

'The bank?'

41

'*The wank-bank,*' he whispered the word, '*wank*' so no one could over hear him.

'I suppose it's a long time passed, and other images replace older ones, fresher ones. Your sex drive declines.'

The waiter returned with their main meals. They ate in silence and finished at the same time. Charlotte smiled at Felix before she spoke.

'Remember Madrid, when I sent you for some condoms, and you were adamant you wanted to try and speak Spanish.'

'To be fair, I did try?'

'You did better than fair.'

'That was my downfall speaking the two sentences I had learnt off by heart so well. But then I got flustered when the older woman behind the counter started speaking to me in machine-gun Spanish, "It is customary in Madrid to only buy condoms for one night's use," The English woman in the queue behind me translated. So I replied with what I thought was three.'

'And how many was it?'

'*Thirty!*'

Charlotte laughed at him, and Felix laughed at himself.

'It's easy to get *tres* and *treinta* mixed up, isn't it?'

She laughed at him again. She tried to remember how long the thirty condoms had lasted them, but couldn't. Their cutlery lay in symmetry pointing at each others'. Twelve o'clock, it was something he had picked up from her, before that he put his knife and fork together, but never in a fixed direction. When she had pointed it out to him, he had quizzed, "But how do you send secret messages to people at the table, if you don't have the clock code?" She thought that was clever, and they had set up their own secret code that only they knew, the end of the knife and the tines were the hands. Twelve was: everything is fine, let's stay here longer. One was: everything is fine, but I'm pissed now. Two was: let's get out of here to somewhere new at the first possible opportunity. Eleven was the food was awful. Ten was let's get straight home and have sex. Three to nine just looked wrong, so they only had five code statements.

'I remember having a silent argument once by pointing at the cutlery. I wanted to carry on and you wanted to go home.' Felix's expression told her he could not recall. 'Are you using the code Felix?'

'Yes, I am sending a message to myself, in case I develop schizophrenia or Alzheimer's in the next few minutes.'

'The code was a good idea. I think it was my idea that.' She giggled at her mischievous lie.

'Yes of course it was, and the Morse code, and you cracked the enigma code as well, and the matrix.'

'That was the best orgasm I ever had in Madrid that holiday, that afternoon when we had a siesta, do you remember that?'

'How do we go from codes to orgasms?'

'A woman's orgasm is a code for most men, one that most never crack. Or just can't be bothered more likely!'

'I thought a team of paramedics were going to rush in and see if you were ok, or possibly the police.'

'*God* that was *amazing*.'

'Do you have a top ten?' Felix asked.

'I have a top one; it makes it easier to remember.'

'Good times.'

'Remember that time with the bread roll at my parent's place?'

'I was a little confused.'

43

'You looked shot at.'

'Well I was confused, I wasn't sure what you had done wrong?'

'Been born, that was the mistake for my mum. *"You must be so embarrassed by her Felix?"* She drawled, your face was a picture, my dad was oblivious. *"Charlotte, how dare you pass the bread roll to Felix with your hands? I do apologise Felix."* You handled her well, as well as anyone can, do you remember what you said?'

'No.'

'You said, *"Charlotte normally has impeccable table manners."* '

'You were always good at placating her. I wanted to say I had my finger on his button last night, just to shut her up.'

'I don't think that would have shut her up somehow. I would have had to have been diplomatic again and inform her, you were just checking my prostate, biggest killer of men between.' Charlotte laughed before he finished. 'Do you think your mum liked me?'

Charlotte sipped her wine and pondered for a short while, looked like she was going to pass comment and cogitated a little longer.

'She doesn't like herself; that's the problem, but will never do anything about her issues.'

'Do you see much of her?'

'Twice a year is all I can manage now. After the first day, sometimes as long as the second, and then we go for each other, too much history. If I see her at a wedding, a funeral, a christening, that's a relief, as there's always an escape from her.'

'She met anyone else?'

'Don't think so, never mentions anyone.'

'I think it's sad.'

44

'That's because *it is sad*, but she won't change, and she leaves me feeling devastated every time we spend any time alone together. You know what she's like, you've had dealings with her... Anyway, let's not talk about my mother. I saw your dad on a documentary, he still looks good for his age?'

'Yeah, he did a piece for Horizon, about how memory is changeable and we edit and change it, then we shape it to what we think has happened exactly. A bit about evolutionary biological memory as well. It's quite easy to manipulate the mind. The red balloon investigation shows that quite well?'

'The mind is a brittle object, when it is not malleable.'

'Life is full of contradictions.'

Felix had a gulp on his water and Charlotte poured herself a glass of water and sipped from it.

'You make out that your work is a bit dull, but it must have its perks?'

'Yeah of course, especially when I first got the gig. I liked the hobnobbing and name dropping, but once that novelty has worn off, when you realise that celebrities are just normal people, that most don't really want to know you unless there is something in it for them...'

'Sounds a bit jaded for you.'

'It's not cynicism. People have busy lives', and why are they going to spend it with someone they hardly know? As you get older, it becomes harder to make friends. That's why it's best to have friends before you are famous; then you know they are true friends, and not along for the ride. Not that I'm in the famous camp, I hardly ever get recognised, and if I didn't do the odd thing on telly, no one would really know me, that picture in *The Times* looks like I'm going to use it for a dating agency...'

45

'Not sure if that's true. The barmaid recognised you when you came in.'

'Not sure about that.'

'Who's the most famous person you have met?'

'How do you gauge that?'

'Uhm, just name drop a few and I will be the judge?'

'Remember!'

She tapped the side of her head in a risible mini salute, '*Sorry Your Honour.*'

'I've met a lot of famous people, especially at parties. I did a load of charity interviews for the *Save the Children Fund*. Everybody gave their time freely, and I only had one stipulation–they were not allowed to talk about the field they were famous for. It was amazing how keen celebrities were to *not* talk about the same things they get questions about day in day out.'

'OK, who is the most interesting person you have met?'

'Nelson Mandela is probably the most famous person. It was only twenty minutes a long time ago, but I felt I was in the company of greatness. A real Saint, what he did for South Africa, gives hope to the whole world, he was so humble.'

'*Now that is* impressive.'

'Yeah, it was amazing. When he'd been whisked out of the room, me and the photographer, John, we just looked at each other and we were speechless. It was like we had been touched by his greatness, his aura; the miasma that's around him just infects you. I was fine in the interview. We went out onto the terrace at The Commons and had a whiskey each. It does not make sense unless you had been in his company.'

'I understand what you mean. What did you ask him?'

'I just told him about what I was trying to achieve, how the profits would go to help children in poverty and the displaced. He'd been briefed by his own people already. He was off immediately talking about how children are the hope of the future. You just believed him; it was like you had no doubt in his words. He talked briefly about education, embracing change, about how he disliked Rugby Union while in Robben Island, because the guards all loved it. How the Rugby World Cup and the honesty trials started to heal a scarred nation.'

'And are children the future?'

'Nelson said they are. Who am I to disagree with the great Madiba?'

'*Wow*, that is one for the grandchildren.'

'Certainly, ' *Resentment is like drinking poison and then hoping it will kill your enemies.*' That's the quote that stayed with me, has always stayed with me.'

'So, you try not to resent things and people?'

'It consumes you if you do. Depends on the severity I suppose. Not easy if you have survived a Japanese or Nazi concentration camp, and most of your family have perished. If Mandela can forgive his white oppressive captors, that is where hope springs from.'

'What about me Felix?' Charlotte tried to catch him while he was feeling philanthropic; at least while he was thinking that way–while he might put her wrong-doing into some form of perspective.

'Nelson would have known!'

She smiled at him, at the thought of it.

47

'Nelson would forgive me, he would tell you to, *"stop wasting my time Felix."* She put on his accent, it was a reasonable effort.

'That's quite good.'

'I'm quite good at pretending to be a dead Saint! Everyone has a hiccup though.'

'No comment, you're trying to influence the judge and jury unduly.'

'Sorry Your Honour. Who else, name dropper?'

'Christopher Hitchens is the cleverest and most interesting person I have ever met and worked with. I wrote to him speculatively just after I finished Uni and he said he would pay me a small retainer to help him do some research on Thomas Jefferson and Henry Kissinger. Still bumped into him until his death, we fell out over his stance on the Iraq War and him publically backing Blair. We had a big argument, which was pretty stupid really. Without his vast umbrella knowledge I'm not sure I would have had the confidence to start writing my column. I got that gig on the back of working for him. I think he put a word in, but he always said he didn't.'

'I don't see you arguing with anyone Felix; you are too laid back, too laissez faire.'

'Oh I'm on the side of truth and honour, and truth and honour is not about greed and exploitation, that's the only time I ever fall out with anyone. I had a real ding dong with Thatcher a long time ago about General Pinochet, how she could defend him, after what he'd done, but then again she supported Botha and therefore Apartheid...'

'Thatcher...' Charlotte teased.

'What about her?'

'That was one of your few buttons that could be pressed, light the Tory blue touch paper. You really hated her, never really got it?'

48

'That's because you came from privilege and it was the rich she always protected. She bloody destroyed community in this country. Don't get me started on the unions. She set a lot of people on the road to selfishness, self-indulgence, and the irony is successive governments, including Tory ones, have to try and undo it, the naivety of the peop–'

'Ok tiger, calm down. Let's move away from politics… *Thatcher!'*

Charlotte let out a giggle and Felix smiled and scowled at her in unequal measure.

'So Charlotte, let's talk about you, you've got fifteen years to fill me in on. You seem to have fallen off the planet in various places. Gone rogue.'

Charlotte looked nervous and sipped on her wine. She looked down at the table cloth, played the dessert spoon in her hand, lingered and fixed Felix with a timid look. It is something she had thought about long and hard. How much to tell him? In the end she decided she would tell him the whole truth. She had toyed with being economical, but she knew if he told Trist about their meeting, he would put him straight and fill in the missing gaps. She now thought herself on trial even more, at least in need of some form of closure, *'the truth, the whole truth and nothing but the truth, so help me God,'* she did not know what the affirmation version was; not that it mattered.

'How much do you know already?'

'I know Giles saw you working in a titty-bar in Hong Kong fifteen years ago. That was the last I heard of you in any detail. Trist never talks about you, not to me anyway.'

'I went to Hong Kong to learn Mandarin. I was teaching Spanish and French at the University, but I only had part time work and the standard of the students' language skills were pretty basic. It was boring in essence. That's where I met Steven; he was teaching Philosophy, couple of years older than me, went to Edinburgh. He was quite boho, and he was earning extra money working in an exclusive bar for rich Hong Kongese women; shirtless with a bow tie, but he was making silly money giving them massages and extras; which is what they *really* wanted. So I did the same, just topless to start with, no extras but the money was great, and it was a good laugh, a good way to meet people. Then after about two months I started doing extras as well…'

'What does *extras as well* entail?'

'Nothing dangerous, pretty basic stuff, always safe, always with a condom. I'd earn more from one night of extras than I did for a week in the bar and the work at the University–The Uni work was really badly paid.'

'Wow.'

Charlotte took a drag on her wine. She registered the surprise on his face and continued anyway.

'By this point Steven and I had moved in. There seemed little point paying rent on two places and I didn't know many people, and he knew lots. He'd been there for nearly two years by this time. Then one night a rich Australian came in the bar, throwing money around, not a faker, and said he wanted a mistress. We sat in his apartment after we had had sex and it was like a business meeting. He told me what he wanted and I told him the terms I wanted, and that was the business deal completed. And that's what I have done ever since, until recently that is, when I got out, as I had made enough money to retire.'

'Wow again.'

'It is not quite as mad as it first sounds. A little shocking maybe, a given for an Oxford graduate with

50

a first in Spanish and French, but a girl has to make a living!'

Felix was shocked. He could see why Trist might have kept her life a secret to him.

'How long were you with Australian man, what did Australian man do to make his mega dollars?'

'I was with him for two years, but the thing you have to remember was, I hardly ever had to go over to Australia, but when he was on business in Hong Kong, I was his only... He made his money in mining, or at least his family did and he inherited it.'

'What are you doing in between?'

'I'm still working at the University. That's what he thinks I'm doing. I'm still living with Steve, and I am only doing big jobs in Hong Kong. I left the topless bar; he would have found out.'

'And Steve is cool with this?'

'Uhm, yes, we made a plan, I would do it for ten years and then I would stop. Steve was still making good money, not in the same league as what I was earning, but we were very comfortable.'

'Is it vulgar to ask how much money?'

'It is vulgar, and you know it, but for example, as a part of the two year deal with the Australian businessman–'

'Do you never use their real names?'

'That's what they are paying me for, *discretion*. It would not do for their wives to find out. I would be ruined and so would their marriages...'

Felix focused on the expression, *'I would be ruined!'* It made her sound like a high class Victorian prostitute. He thought about asking for some clarification, but he did not want to stop her flow. Instead he acknowledged her with an *'Umm.'*

'Part of the deal was a small two bedroom flat over-looking the harbour in Balmain. So after two

51

years, we owned a flat in Sydney and we had paid for a two bedroom flat in Hong Kong. By the age of twenty five I joint owned two apartments in two of the most expensive cities in the world for real estate.'

'*Wow.* So you said you had ground rules, would it be rude to ask what they were?'

'After Australian man, I was moving in very rich circles with him and it was supposed to be a secret, "*our relationship.*" '

Charlotte made rabbit ears for punctuation marks. Felix hated it when people did that, but he ignored it.

'I was in demand, for lots of reasons. I had time to formulate my strategy and rules, there is not much competition in this field of work. Most men want a high class prostitute and variation, it's the lonely married men and innately monogamous that want a companion. Rule one was, it was to last no more than six months, for two reasons. Firstly, if you pick six months, it is not normally enough for most men, and they will lavish you with gifts, or try and bribe you with extra money to keep you a bit longer. I never did more than a year with any man, except the first one. Secondly, six months is bearable if they are odious.'

'How many have there been?'

Without thinking she snapped the answer back at him.

'Fifteen.' She did not give him time to interrogate her on the number, and carried on. 'The second rule, they are not to leave their wives. I'm just a fling, I'm on hire and I'm not forever. Third rule, I don't do pain, I will do dressing up, kinky. They can tie me up, but only if I trust them, a bit of harmless spanking, but no real pain. Pain can lead to danger.'

'Ever get scary?'

'Only once. I was tied down; he'd been sweet until this point. He was using a vibrator on me, and he was doing it harder and harder, had a horrible serial

52

killer look in his eyes. He didn't even fuck me; he just wanted to hurt me. He was taking his pain and frustration out on me. He soon stopped and untied me; I had let him gag me, but when he saw the horror in my eyes and heard my muffled screaming he relented. Then he sat against the wall and cried like a baby. He hurt me both physically and emotionally. Obviously I didn't see him again, and he tried to apologise, sent me some expensive gifts, but I couldn't trust him after that. Still, I did very well from the gifts.'

Felix tried to evaluate if she was being flippant as a defence mechanism. His initial amazement was now turning to genuine intrigue.

'So, were you always based in Hong Kong?'

'No, I flew where the clients wanted me. There was a fourth rule that I didn't share with them, if they ever flew me economy–I called it off and never told them why!'

'What was Steven doing while you were out of the country?'

'He was still teaching; he'd started an MA, he did the odd extras for long term clients, but he was studying and working hard, little time to spare, hoping to step it up for a doctorate.'

'Did you carry on teaching languages?'

'It became too difficult so I did a few withdrawal tutorials ad hoc. I was making more effort with my Mandarin when I had free time, and it was coming on well.'

'How many languages do you speak fluently now?'

'French and Spanish obviously, my Italian and Mandarin are pretty good, and I can get by in Arabic, but I can't write that. Uhm, I sort of learned Esperanto for a bit of a laugh as well.'

'It's very impressive, all the same.'

53

'It's not really impressive, it's just a bit of dedication and a lot of time, that's all you need. Once you learn the grammar rules, a lot just transfer easily.'

'If only it was as simple as that.'

'You speak French. Your French is *très bien*. Would be a lot better if you practiced your avoir and etre a bit more, that's the key.'

'So did speaking Mandarin open many doors so to speak to speak?'

'Yes, it was useful and fun to learn.'

'Isn't Cantonese the main language of Hong Kong?'

'Yes, but not the lingua franca of China, that's Mandarin, and we have The Chairman to thank for the unity of language in The People's Republic.'

'So if you can speak and write four major languages, and speak several others, does that not make you an expert? A global expert almost?'

'Maybe, but how would I explain away all the missing years of non-academia? I really should improve my Arabic, but I have lost interest now.'

'Tell me more about the clients. I am assuming you had an Arabic client and that's why you were learning the language?'

'Two, one about seven years ago, and one about three years ago...'

'Three years ago would take you past your thirty-fourth birthday?'

'Are you Sherlock Holmes, Felix?'

'Just paying attention, rude not to.'
She laughed at him.

'I will come back to that later, but I have stopped, I can assure you of that?'

'OK.'

'Both the Arabs were quite sweet. I know stereotypically they don't always have the best reputation with women.'

Felix chose not to interrupt her flow.

'–It makes you laugh though, one had three wives and the other had four and they still wanted me.'

'*Greedy.*'

'*Very much so.* The first one I was with for six months to the day. Their hand so speak, is their bond. He lavished me when he was in London, which was only three times. When we drove to the airport in a top of the range Rolls for the final time, the driver got out and handed me the keys and the papers. I got the papers signed in my name and sold it immediately to a garage in the West End for over a hundred grand. That's what I mean by lavish; he left me a credit note for forty grand at Cartier's in Chelsea, plus the rest. The second more recent Arab, both from Dubai–both cousins incidentally.'

'Keep it in the family.'

'*Exactly.* He took a real shine to me. Obsessed with A levels, Sheikh Double Lube I used to call him. He got me a two bedroom flat to live in, in Knightsbridge. I only saw him four times in nine months...'

'Breaking the rules.'

'He was holding the flat over me, saying if I stayed with him for three more months he would sign the flat over to me, *if* I set up a legitimate business, so it looked like a bona fide business deal. So I did, or I got an accountant to do it for me. I thought he may renege on the deal, but an Arab's hand shake is not just for slapping your arse, so I found out.'

'So you still got this flat then?'

'Yeah, in the company name, I rent it out through an agency, have no dealings with it really.'

'Were you not tempted to live in it yourself?'

'Not in the country enough. I have a small mews in Camden, which I love. The Knightsbridge flat is too sterile. It's not a home, more a crash-pad.'

'Bloody hell, you're like a property magnet?'

'Mum bought me the mews house when dad died. God knows how much she must have got, insured up to the heavens. I looked on it as compensation for having to have lived with her, and my get out clause from being her daughter.'

'So where is Steve in all this now?'

'We split a few years ago, sort of drifted apart.'

'Tell me more about your salacious life?'

'I know it sounds that way, but it really isn't. Most of my clients were lonely, and they felt obliged to their wives, felt they couldn't leave them out of loyalty. Thing with having mainly older clients is they are not going to go at it all night, they want a quick wham bam and then a cuddle and someone to talk to.'

'How old is old?'

'The oldest I have ever had was seventy.'

'*Seventy,* is that not like sleeping with your Granddad?'

'He was actually very nice, and he knew his way around a woman's body, a kinky devil. It's amazing what Viagra can do. I must admit there were a couple of times when I thought he was going to have a heart attack on me!'

Felix laughed and Charlotte joined in.

'The worst was a New Zealand client. He was a miserable sod, and a tight *Git* as well. He used to e-mail a list of topics he wanted to talk about…'

'Like what?'

'Like Politics, current affairs, art, rugby union– that's all it said once, rugby union. I know nothing about sport, he was referring to the forthcoming World

Cup; needless to say we didn't talk about that much. He took me to a match and it was just him and me in a hospitality box for twelve people. He was not impressed when I said, *"are they just jumping on each other, or is there some strategy to it!"* I was joking, he had a right strop, said I was *"ungrateful."* Six months was enough with him; he had yet another strop when we got to the hotel room and I had brought the wrong French underwear. I had red on, he wanted black.'

'New Zealand colours.'

'Uhm, that might have been it, you should have been my advisor. When we eventually parted company he'd written me a report, and divided it into two sections; what I did well: what I could improve on!' Felix and Charlotte laughed in unison.

'I know,' she said acknowledging their shared amusement.

'Go on, share the half yearly report.'

She laughed before she carried on, and Felix laughed at the anticipation.

'Did well: massage–especially back, fellatio, dress–sophisticated, time keeping–always punctual, never had to wait, choice of restaurants–good standard, excellent knowledge of language and cultures–'

'That degree came in handy then.'

'Oh yes, coming from a man who could speak only one language! Discretion–high standard. But on the negative, room for improvement side: hair not always immaculate.'

'He has a point.'

'Stop right there–my hair is lovely today, I even washed it.'

'I'm joking, it looks great.'

'"More humour needed." I told him he could hire a court jester, and he never even cracked his face.'

Felix laughed aloud, 'That's funny.'

'Firmer breasts.'

'Did he elaborate further?'

'He didn't need to; he wanted them stuck up like two silicon pillows, saluting him. I informed him if I did get them done, *then he* wouldn't see the benefits! But he honestly thought he was doing me a favour, like it was a professional appraisal?'

'Which in a way, it was?'

'It was an appraisal I could have shoved up his arse!'

'He might have liked that?'

'Believe me, he wouldn't have. But it would have looked funny on the 'need to improve' column.'

They both laughed together.

'So what have you had done then?'

'Felix, you don't ask a woman that.'

'*Yeah, yeah,* come on spill the beans?'

'Nothing, nada, rien.'

'You're lying, your head tilts just a little to your dominant right and you can't keep it in, your head either shakes or you spurt out a nervous laugh... there she blows,' Felix pointed at her. 'Just like that, so come on, spill the beans?'

'Around the eyes, just slightly, and my arse lifted a bit, that's it, I swear.'

'Not the titties?'

'No, I have great tits, as you well know, if I had kids I would have had them done maybe, but so far they have pretty much stood the test of time.'

'Best ever present?'

'Flat in Knightsbridge, worth silly money.'

'Worst ever present?'

58

'Footspa.'

'Seriously, *a footspa*?'

'Yeah one client bought me a footspa!'

'What country was he from?'

'Hong Kong, incidentally, the worst place to have a client or anywhere both of you live, they pop around and pester you for blow jobs!'

They both laughed at the thought of it.

'Worst place visited?'

'Mexico City. Felt like I was going to get killed constantly, even in the hotel room, which was next to the police station.'

'Best City lived in?'

'Sydney—sun always shone, over-looked the harbour, food was great, and had a naughty bit on the side when Ozzie man was not around.'

'Best meal?'

'Paros, Greece. Are you trying to trick me?'

'Worst meal?'

'Shanghai, I don't know what it was, but I wouldn't have liked to have met it when it was alive, if it was as fierce as it was revolting to eat. Expensive is not always better for the Chinese, believe me.'

'Most bizarre thing asked to do?'

'Pretend to be a blow up doll, and squeak while in coitus!'

'Tell me more.'

'I got the impression he thought he was in a dream, rather than a fantasy, and before he was very rich he more than likely had an inflatable friend that came to life at nights.'

'Sorry, I just have to ask this...How do you pretend to be a blow up doll?'

She banged her forehead with the palm of her hand, *'cling-film stupid.'* And they both laughed and attracted the attention of several diners and the headwaiter.

'How do you get into the cling film?'

'He wrapped me in it. It was not the first time he'd done it, believe me.'

Felix was trying to picture Charlotte wrapped in cling film and how tricky it must be.

'Could you move your arms?'

'Yeah, he wrapped them separately. He wanted to put it over my head and cut holes in, like he had done below. But you have to draw the line somewhere; some things are even embarrassing in death.'

'Did you do the squeaking noises?'

'I tried, but it was so hilarious, I started giggling. He asked me to stop, but, I'm assuming you have never tried to stop laughing when covered in cling film, while pretending to be an inflatable woman, have you, Felix?'

'I imagine it could be quite difficult.'

'It certainly was, but I tell you one thing it is good for, weight loss, after a bit of hanky-panky in cling film, the sweat starts to pour from you.'

'Do you look good in cling film Charlie?' He smiled as he said it.

'I look good in most things, but I looked better before I started sweating like a dog in a Chinese restaurant.'

'Make the squeaking noise?'

'No, not here.'

'Go on, squeak for me, squeak, squeaky. Squeak like a lady-doll!'

'No Felix.'

'*Remember…* You're on trial.'

She looked embarrassed. She looked around at the other diners, to make sure they were not looking at her. She leaned towards Felix and let out two quiet

60

squeaky mouse sounds, the second higher than the first. Felix started first, unable to control himself. He tried to keep it in, but it was no use. He matched the squeaking up to the image of Charlotte pretending to be a human blow-up doll, swaddled in elastic polymer and sweating. Once he was off, she followed suit, coupled in hysterics, attracting the attention of quite a lot of the patrons. The head waiter walked across towards them, and they tried hard to check themselves. When he appeared by the table, they were only just starting to regain some control again. Charlotte was waving an arm at him in a form of non-verbal apology.

'Would Sir or Madam like dessert?'

'Not for me.'

'Not for me either.' They both forced out.

'Can you keep our bill open? We would like to withdraw to the bar, that's ok, isn't it?' Now slightly more composed, then she let a latent suppressed giggle escape, Felix had to laugh along.

'Certainly, would you like coffee?'

'Hold the coffees for now.'

Charlotte inspected the wine bottle with only three inches left in the bottom. She poured it into her glass and stood up slowly, making sure she would be steady when she did so. Felix poured the last of the water in his glass and started to follow Charlotte to the bar area. Halfway across the restaurant towards the door Charlotte stopped and a look of horror flashed across her face.

'What is it Charlie?'

'Oh my God, my bag, I left my bag under the table!'

She walked back agitated, pulled it from under the table and clutched it close to her chest and smiled at Felix, relieved. Felix thought it was a little over dramatic. Of all the places to leave your bag, Claridge's would be one of the safest in the world. What was so precious in there? It was a hassle if you had to cancel lost cards, lost phone contacts. He was pleased to see the look of reassurance on her face, as she neared him.

'Come on you numpty.' He said to her as she drew up to him with her bag and a glass of wine in the other hand.

The bar was just as empty as before, and they sat on the same bar stools, away from other drinkers.

'High end prostitute at the other end of the bar, waiting for a client to arrive from a business meeting. He will come into the bar and look around; pretend the person he is looking for is not here, surreptitiously make eye contact with her and vice versa, and then go up to his room, suite probably, she will walk confidently over to the lift and disappear.'

'You don't know that.'

'Trust me, designer twin set, black killer stilettos. Look at the size of that bag, for all the miscellaneous items she might need up stairs, red lipstick, legs waxed like marble, I will put money on it!'

'Ok, hundred quid to charity.'

'Ok.'

They shook hands.

'Remember a hand shake is a bond, not just for slapping arses.'

She blushed and laughed it off.

'Tell me the truth about Steve? You wanted to brush it off before, there is more to it, isn't there?'

'No, not really.'

'You're lying, I know you are.' He probed with his eyes.

'Ok, but don't repeat any of what I have told you. Don't gossip about me, and don't write about me in your column. I have been totally honest with you.'

'Why wouldn't you be?'

'You know, sometimes it's better to be economical with the truth, for lots of reasons, like the time in the river at Lady Margaret's.'

'I assume you are not always this honest?'

'It would be a fair assumption, *yes.*'

'Is there something more profound you want to tell me? Is that why you are being so honest with me?'

'Like what?'

'I don't know, are you ill, or have you done something really bad?'

'No, there's nothing wrong. I just feel with you I don't need to hide anything, or play games, what's the point, far too much history between us.'

'Are you sure?'

'No, nothing is wrong, silly.'

'You *really* sure, yeah?'

'Yes, sure, nothing is wrong.'

'So tell me what happened with Steven?'

Charlotte sipped her drink and looked at Felix before she spoke. The barman appeared, and before he could enquire to their order, she informed him, 'Bottle of Moet thanks.'

Felix told her off with his rolled eyes.

'Don't say it, you boring git. *I can't drink anymore I have an interview to do.* I bet the DP cries off. Another hundred quid says he does.'

'Ok, you're on.'

They shook hands on it.

'Steven, *remember?*'

'Ok, I didn't treat him very well, quite badly in fact. I got a bit depressed. It was all fantastic to start with, the plan was going well. There was always an exit strategy. We wanted the same things, have some fun, make loads of money, then get out, retire to the sun, or at least have the option. It was not long before we had another apartment in Hong Kong. Then we started buying properties in North West Italy, Liguria, on the coast mainly, pumping any spare money into them; interest only mortgages, just to get the properties. We set up a limited company there, everything in joint names. We were happy. Thirty-three max and then I was stopping. Then I got a bit depressed; it was just after my dad died. I was devastated, as you can imagine.'

Charlotte welled with emotion, and swigged the last of her wine from the meal. Felix thought she was about to cry and he rubbed the top of her arm affectionately.

'Thanks, sorry; he was my life, you know. He was a lovely man, great father, why he ended up being tortured by her, I'll never work out?'

'You ok?'

'Yeah, just my dad and maybe how I treated Steven… If I'm honest, you as well?'

'Ok, yeah?' He placed his arm by his side.

'Why didn't I stay with you Felix? I would have been poor, but I would have had a shot at happiness.'

'You would never have been poor, that has never been an option for you.'

'You may have had to have done a few years of nine til five, but poor, not in the script.'

'You know when I was at my very, very happiest, ever?'

'Not dressed as a blow up doll, at a guess.'

She smiled at him and her eyes glazed over.

'Back at Margaret's with you in my room and we would play footsie on the big red settee, you reading at one end, me at the other, the soles of our feet massaging each other's, until we could stand it no longer, when one of us got bored with studying, to see who would crack first, then…'

'*Do you want to shag?*'

'We never said *no*, not once, ever, do you know that? Then we would read in bed, until someone got bored again, and we would be at it again. That's what I miss most, that room, us, that moment in time, and for some reason I had to destroy it, destroy us, *why did I do that?*'

Felix started to stir with emotion. He tried to dissolve the room from his mind. It was something that was fantastic at the time, but now it had passed a long time ago. He had moved on, left all that behind in Oxford, left her behind.

'I've been a fucking idiot with love Fe. I have destroyed good men, tainted them, *sorry…*'

'Some things are not meant to be, time and a place. If we had stayed together, I would not have kids, and I cannot imagine my life without them now.'

She contemplated his words for a moment, and then added.

'What you've never had, you never miss. Sorry I need the toilet, I need to−'

He interrupted her before she could continue. 'I need the toilet as well. Let's rendezvous here, unless I pick up the prostitute on the way back?'

'*Sorry*, *again*, meet you back here in a minute.'

Felix returned first from the toilet and when he did the woman at the opposite end of the bar had gone. Charlotte returned and smiled at him.

'I asked her?'

'Rubbish, you're lying, you wouldn't do that, not in your nature.'

'I asked her.' He tried to sound more convincing.

'Utter rubbish…'

65

'You were right… she's a prostitute.'

'She was gone when you got back, wasn't she?, and even if you had asked her, she would have lied to you if she was turning tricks.'

'So, Steven?'

'Ok, but don't judge me, not you Fe, *yeah*, you're better than that*, please?*'

'Ok, promise.'

'My dad died and I was lost, and a long way from home, and the thought of coming home to the house, without him there… *well*… I just couldn't face it. I started taking too much coke, E's and drinking too much, not sleeping well. I was having a break from work, I couldn't work anyway, my head wasn't right. I tried to drive him away. We got married–I forgot to tell you that. We went to New York. It was a mad week, took a few friends with us, and had a great time. I have always been somewhat insecure–you always knew that, even when you met me, like you said, you thought you could tame me. He thought exactly the same, anyway–'

Felix broke in. 'When I saw you that first day, *God you were beautiful, carefully tableauxed*. Reading that pretentious book, enticing the men in, moths to the flame. I could see what you were doing, and it was obvious, you knew, but not many others did. You knew how enchanting you were. I knew it was a game you were playing. I knew I would eventually get my turn, but I had to play it canny, or I would have been one of the fallen riders. So, I deliberately gave you a wide birth, made no effort, never sat with you at dinners. While you shagged around, you had a right reputation you know?'

'I know, I was naive and insecure and I loved the attention, especially coming from an all-girls school. I wish I could turn back the clock, but it was

66

sexual freedom and the pill I blame... never myself, *obviously.*'

He knew she was being flippant, thought she might smile at her own pseudo-self-effacing analysis, but when she didn't he said. 'And that's why you had a go at me that night when you were pissed, because I was not giving you the attention you desired. You tried so hard that year.'

'I know, it's ridiculous thinking back.'

'On the way down from NEW-*castle* with my mum and dad in the car–'

'Say *Newcastle* again?'

'NEW-caastle.'

'You can take the boy out of Newcastle, but... What I hated about you, your northern assured good-looking contended provincialness, is what I came to love. What a paradox hey?'

'When I saw you sat there reading Tolstoy, it reminded me of a song I had heard on Radio Two on the way down, a Randy Crawford tune about men wanting this woman in the song because she was adorable and life held no fear for her. I saw you and I thought, you *lucky-thing*. I heard it a few months after we had split up and it made me cry, it shot me back, you know...'

Charlotte rubbed his thigh. 'Sorry.'

'It's fine, these are the honesty trials, or so it seems?'

'Yeah, something like that.'

'So Steven?' He realised too much alcohol had caused him to break into her speech about her husband, or maybe it was ex-husband now?

'The trial continues, what would Kafka make of it all? So dad died, and I was a bit of a mess. He thought everything would be fine–he's an optimist like you. So I drove him away.'

67

She fixed him a stare. He glanced back, accused with his eyes, knowing she was holding back.

'*What?*' She countered.

'There is something else, something you're not telling me?'

'After fifteen years, you think you can still read me?'

'After a lifetime I could tell, and a reincarnation as well.'

'Ok, *in for a penny…* On my thirty-third birthday, when it was supposed to stop. He's watched the calendar for years, counting down the days, when I would be only his and vice versa, no more sharing whatsoever. He didn't mind it to start with, but I think psychologically when you hit thirty, definitely when I hit thirty, it started to bother him more. The plans you make in your twenties are different to those you make in your thirties. A friend of the mining Australian offered me a great deal with an apartment or money, but it was only a six month contract. It was such a great offer. This is before the Knightsbridge apartment–I would have not been interested then. I would be based in Darwin; his family were based in Perth. Margot was still there at that time, and property prices were starting to rocket due to the booming mining business. I played hard to get. Truth be told, he was quite good looking and I liked the attention. This was to be the *very last* client. I should have got out. I had plenty of money. I got greedy, too greedy to be honest, maybe a little institutionalised, *maybe?* This was the very last of the pension, the last of the easy money. But Steven got really upset; he'd never got this upset before, said if I didn't stop now, it would never end. I took the offer anyway–it was for both of us. I always shared the money fifty-fifty. I'd never hidden anything from him. But Steve was adamant

68

that I shouldn't do it. By this time we had four properties in Italy, plus the rest.'

'So what did he do?'

'He gave me an ultimatum. He said if I took it, we were over and he went off to Italy. He had a doctorate by this stage. I knew that when the six months were over I would sell the apartment or take the money. I would come home with the big pay cheque, smooth things out between us, and that was the last one. It would have paid for more than two of the smaller properties in Italy out-right. I just looked on it as a last business deal.'

'But it was not the last one?

'No, but it probably would have been.'

'Probably?'

'Anyway, but when I got to Italy he was still pissed with me. He'd never stamped his feet before– this was the very first time. We had befriended an English couple that lived next door to the house we always stayed in. He was very friendly with them when I got there. So we amicably split everything except my property in London down the middle.'

'Then what?'

'What do you mean?'

'What did you do after the split?'

Charlotte further filled both their glasses to the top with champagne, before Felix could protest.

'He will cry off, and his wife will find out about another affair, but not before the media do.'

'Do you want a wager on that?'

'I will need good odds. Come on, it's been fifteen years. What if it's another fifteen years. You will regret not staying longer.''

'Ok, but I'm sipping like the lady you should be.'

69

She smiled at him, 'I can be a lady, but not around you. I never had to be false around you. Another toast, to you this time, something nice to toast to, something splendid.'

Felix thought for a moment.

'To the memory of your dad, top bloke.'

Charlotte started to well up.

'Oh Fe, *you lovely, lovely man*. Thanks, ok.'

She hoisted her glass into the air, and Felix clipped his against it.

'To your dad.' 'To dad.'

She rubbed his arm.

'So let's have the truth, the real truth, and nothing but–not what you think you can get away with?'

'Ok, don't judge me, *yes,* you promised?'

'Only God...'

Charlotte took a gulp of her drink and seemed to mentally steady herself.

'I slept with his friend next door.'

'What?'

'*No judging*, I thought he was knocking off the girl-friend, and he was being so frosty. I got jealous; I know I had no right to. I was drinking far too much, sat around in the sun, and I seduced the man next door, and that *really* fucked things up, literally and figuratively. I was angry with him, angry that he might be strong enough to just walk away from us. I was not in control I suppose. That's why we split up, and split everything, well almost everything down the middle.'

'*Wow, that's really bad.*'

'*Felix*, stop it.'

'I'm embarrassed enough as it is. I might have to start lying if you are going to be judgemental.'

'Sorry, but it sort of hit me from the azzuro.'

'Why do I do it Fe?'

'It's a syndrome. You feel secure with men, but that eventually makes you feel insecure. You know they love you, but because you want every man to love you, you drive away the close ones, the doting ones. It is a syndrome, especially prevalent in woman that have always been successful, but then fail at something. It usually manifests itself by the women choosing awful men that treat them *really* badly…'

'You're making this up?'

'No, there is such a syndrome. Not *my* theory, *a theory*.'

'But I always choose the most wonderful men and drove them away; that does not fit into your theory?'

'Maybe you are trying to replicate the love of your own father. Maybe you wanted to carry on being the professional mistress–you had attention lavished upon you by lots of men, and you got paid extremely well in the process. Maybe you had outlived him; you can be very fickle with love?'

'I used to be fickle, not any more–this was the final straw.'

Felix was trying to decide if she had changed; or they were just drunken words to make her sound better, reformed–still the recidivist. Surely everyone changes, grows into something new, for better or for worse, mainly better?

'I wasn't moving on. I didn't have anyone to go to.'

'That's probably unusual. Most insecure people nearly always have someone to go to, a crutch.'

'So you got a theory about that?'

'You're an enigma, because even though you are insecure in relationships, you are very confident as well, you have had confidence bred into you, the best

71

school, the best university, etc... So where did you go after the split?'

'I went to London.'

'Why?'

'*You know why?*'

'You carried on didn't you?'

She smiled at him.

'Yeah, I had had an offer from the second Arab.'

'That's why you didn't mention the property in the split?'

'You should have been a detective Felix.'

'I might've had to have been if I'd carried on going out with you. So have you stopped now?'

'Yes, I stopped three years ago.'

'So what do you do with your days?'

'There are plenty of things to fill the day.'

'Like what?'

'I read lots, shop, beautify myself. I go out with Jodi from school. I always kept in touch with Jodi, she lives in London now.'

'Kids?'

'Yes, two.'

'So she is busy a lot, yeah?'

'There is something else I am not proud of.'

'Come on, spit it out.'

'I just left a bit out, lied. His best friend came over to Italy. Lovely guy–Jamie, we got really pissed one night after he'd been there for about a week. Everything was very comfortable and relaxed. We were all really pissed and Steven went to bed and Jamie and I had sex, drunken sex. My back was aching from sorting the garden out and the rubbing led to–'

'*Fucking?*'

Charlotte sipped her drink.

'Yes, something like that, but it was just drunkenness, the alcohol acting out. I told him it was just a one off, but he wanted more. He knew the writing was on the wall for Steven and I. Steven had told him. He was single. I said *no* repeatedly, but he wouldn't take *no* for an answer. I told him it was getting beyond a joke now. We had an argument that Steven overheard and the shit well and truly hit the fan.'

'Bloody hell Charlie.'

'I know, I'm my own worst enemy. *I have* changed now. I'm going to meet the right man and I am going to treat him right. Play nice.'

'Right, was the next door neighbour before or after Jamie?'

Charlotte put her drink to her lips and tilted her head to one side slightly, without drinking she smiled and replied with the glass slightly magnifying her lips, '*before.'*

'*Wow,* so all the joint plans evaporated?'

'Pretty much so, yes.'

'Would there be any chance that he would take you back, do you think?'

'Not now no. I respect him for that, why should he? The thing is we both did very well out of the previous eleven years together. Neither of us need ever work again, if we so chose.'

'But there must have been future plans, with all the money. You weren't going to sit around for the next forty years drinking red wine and martinis on the veranda, *surely?'*

'Yes, we had plans, all revolved around Italy. We talked of opening a complex, like a retreat almost, that had a top restaurant in, with a top chef, yoga, language school, painting classes, something like that. We were going to look into that, find the right location.

73

I was keen on a high end hotel for businessmen, but Steven was vehemently against it.'

'*High end business hotel?* By that you mean a high end brothel.'

Charlotte laughed as she put the glass to her lips, but did not reply.

'What about Steven and Jamie, have they made up?'

'Not sure, wasn't looking good the last time I saw them.'

'And the last time you saw them, Jamie was tag teaming you with the next door neighbour.'

Charlotte laughed at him and played with her hair at the same time. She would have been angry if someone else had said it.

'It was not like that. I know it sounds *really* bad, but I think it was all to do with my dad dying–a reaction to it.'

'And the drink?'

'Yes, that didn't help, but that was down to my dad dying as well, especially the next day, alcohol never used to make me depressed the next day, but...'

'You must have a mini plan now?'

'I need to move on from my past life first, get it out of my system–'

'But you said that you stopped three years ago?'

'Uhm, yes I did... but there are no self-help books on this sort of thing. I never thought I would say this, but I think I might see a counsellor about my life, my dad's death, my mother, and my relationships. I'm not proud of what I did. But I have changed a lot. I think it is like a lot of people when they are young; they have to have a few relationships before they find the one they can settle down with. If you just stay with your childhood sweet-heart all your life, you are always going to have itchy feet, and wonder if the grass is greener on the other side.'

'When did you really stop the work? It was not three years ago was it?'
Felix threw her a critical look and she tried to dodge it.

'Yes, about three years ago, maybe a bit less.'

'You're lying, I can tell. Why tell the truth about everything else, but not this?'

'Ok, two years ago… *a year ago*. I was bored so I thought I might as well make some money at the same time.'

'I double-dated for those two years, but I stopped one year ago. That's the truth, *honest.*'

'Ok, so now the plan is?'

'I want to meet a man and have children.'

'You said you *never* wanted children, *ever?*'

'People change. I was young, I thought that was what I wanted—call it naivety if you like?'

'That was one of the reasons that made the heartache more bearable for me, knowing you didn't want to have children. I didn't want to have children then, but I knew subconsciously one day I would. I suppose I wanted the option. You were always so definite. It could have caused problems.'

'The circle of life—'

'And it keeps on turning.'

Charlotte smiled. 'As you mature, you understand why children are so important. It's your link to the past and your link with the future, maybe it's biological programming, a computer virus. You can fight it for so long, but it always wins. You have to leave a copy of yourself. I feel I have the skills and the love to give to a child now. We both know the real reason I didn't want to have kids, but I have dealt with that, and patterns do not have to repeat themselves.'

'So where are you going to meet this man with the super-sperm?'

'I've been on some computer agency dates, but most have been time wasters, just want a shag.'

'Try before you buy?'

Charlotte laughed at him and sipped her champagne and giggled again.

'I don't think they wanted to buy, more like shoplifting.'

'You must have lots of contacts from your previous life, surely?'

'Yes, but I can't shack up with one of them. Imagine the scandal and gossip. I need someone away from there. I'm in a fortunate position, that I'm not constrained by money, so if I met someone special I wouldn't have to rely on him for financial support. The problem is the ones I meet my age and a bit older, all seem to be old before their time, and ones younger, just seem so immature, so young, lacking in life skills and experience. Then you throw kids in the mix, I don't want to look after someone else's kids, be the evil step-mum?'

'You might be good at that?'

She giggled at him and he smiled back.

'That's what I'm worried about, *'Hi kids, Dr Vodka is coming around later, so you need to go to bed early tonight'* '

'I will have to go soon, you know that?'

'You could cancel; it's been fifteen years Fe. We still have lots to catch up on. You can rearrange your meeting.'

Felix thought about it for a moment, while Charlotte cajoled him to stay. He pulled his phone out of his jacket and scrolled down his contacts. He pressed the screen and wandered to a quieter part of the bar. Charlotte watched with fixed anticipation as he chatted

76

away, while nodding his head, he rocked back and forth on his ankles. He walked back and smiled at her.

'What's the scores on the doors then?'

'I've cancelled it... The Deputy was running late anyway and he could only give me fifteen minutes maximum.'

'Excellent.' She broke into a smile as she said it. 'Do you remember that boat party your PPE lot threw on the Thames?'

'It was funny, poetic justice I suppose. What was that Bully Boy called, *Urquhart*.'

'I used to call him '*haircut one hundred*.' He hated that didn't he?'

'No, you called him *haircut one hundred pence*, just to annoy him.'

She laughed. 'That's right; he actually called me an *oik* once!'

'I bet you called him something a little more Anglo-Saxon?'

She smiled, but could not remember her rejoinders.

'Horrible boy. A real slug.'

'To be fair, he hated a lot of things too numerous to mention.'

'How did we end up just outside the terrace bar on the river anyway?'

'One of the rich kids bribed the captain to go further down the river than he was supposed to.'

'That's right, then the mooning started.'

'Oh yeah, started by you and Margot if I remember rightly?'

'I blame Trist, I think he started it, actually.'

'You and Margot didn't need much encouraging.'

'It was funny when William R mooned his dad, and before he noticed it was him, his dad had shouted, '*arrest those louts,*' they both chorused together and laughed.

'I remember when the river police boarded and you and Margot kissed the first officer on board on his cheeks simultaneously.'

'And Margot absolutely pissed said, *'have you come to take down our particulars?'*'

'The funniest bit was when William R saw it was his dad remonstrating red faced, the penny dropped and, William shouted, *"abort parliament jape."'* They both chorused again and laughed.

"*Abort parliament jape."* He was a pompous wanker, wasn't he?'

'Still is, the irony now being, he convinced twenty-three thousand people to vote for him in a Tory safe seat. Now he is sat on the Terrace Bar looking out on the river at the common people.'

Charlotte smiled in recognition of that hot June summer's day. It was the first summer they had gone out and then the next day they had flown over to Felix's parents' place in France. Charlotte had one of the worst hangovers, if not the worst hangover she could remember. She kept dry-retching into a carrier bag, and Felix had to tell people she had, '*a bit of food poisoning.*' They nearly didn't let her on the plane. Then when they got there, Felix's mum kept saying, ''Is she pregnant, Felix?''

'Messing about on the river.' He reminisced.

'Now you would be off to Guantanamo Bay being water-boarded.'

'*Abort Parliament jape*, I said it to him once on the Terrace when he was sat with Marcus, and he asked me to keep my voice down.'

'What did you say?'

'I told him it was a vote winner, connecting with the electorate–smashing up restaurants was not. He

78

tried to ignore me and he had that look of disapproval on his face, that: *"How did you ever get to do PPE at Oxford with the likes of us?"'*

'It feels like today is a new start for me. Meeting you Fe, after so long, *hopefully* getting some redemption. I said *hopefully*, before you get on your high judicial horse.'

'That's good that you are feeling so positive, save you a fortune in shrinks fees?'

'Uhm.'

'So tell me about your wife. Where did you meet, all the details?'

'We met in a comedy club.'

'Jongleurs?'

'Yeah, good guess, *Jongleurs.* She was carrying some drinks from the bar, and I turned round to find Arran, who was down for the weekend for an England match. I knocked her drink and most of it spilled. I apologised, offered to buy her another. She wasn't that bothered. It was three deep at the bar, so she said 'next time you queue up get me one then', so I did and I took it over to her and her friends.'

'…And clumsiness.'

'Yeah, poor co-ordination.'

'Was she one of the acts, *a comedienne*?'

'Used to be after university–she did a degree at Leeds Met in creative writing, and then went and did an MA in Comedy Performance at Kent Universit–'

'You can get an MA in comedy?'

'Only if you're funny!'

Charlotte laughed at him.

'Abi did stand up for a few years, did the circuit. She said she was great at the performing, but found it hard to come up with new material all the time, especially when she was the *compere* at a pub in Islington–when lots of the same people came back week in week out. So after a few years, just before she met me, she started being a part time agent for some of her friends. Then it snowballed, and because she was in at the ground floor and people trusted her, she started taking bookings, helping out at gigs, schmoozing, keeping all parties happy. Two of her acts are pretty big, and it's ideal now we have the kids. She can work from home whenever she chooses. I don't need to be in the office every day, so one of us can always be there, especially if the kids are ill. The nursery they used to go to was a nightmare. The slightest sign of diarrhoea or an infection, and they made you keep them at home. If they got the shits, you had to have them at home for three days after–I'm sure they had some kind of sensitive shit viscosity detector. I'm at home as well quite a bit at the moment; you waste an hour and a half of the day commuting. So we are not like a lot of our friends who sit down for tea between seven and eight, don't see their kids before they go to bed. We have a good routine, which is important.'

'What's that Geordie thing you used to call kids?'

'Wee bairns.'

Charlotte smiled at him.

'That's it, *the wee bairns.*'

She made an appalling attempt.

'Remember you always made me watch '*The Likely Lads*', when it was on. You used to love that.'

'Used to? You canne stop liking '*The Likely Lads*', *pet.*'

'The part where one of them is fishing–'

'Terry–'

'And the other one turns up–'

'Bob–'

80

'And Bob says to Terry, "Can I have one of your cans of lager?" And Terry says, "Sorry mate, I've only got three left." '

They both laughed.

'What are your kids called again?'

'Futon and Issy, short for Islington, because that's where they were both conceived.'

'You're joking right?'

'Yeah, Sam and Eva. Sam after her granddad, and Eva after my grandma.'

'Is your granny still alive?'

'No, she died ten years ago.'

'Oh.'

'We had a nightmare with names. In the end they were the compromises we settled on.'

'What is Abi like?'

'Intelligent, organised, self-effacing, trust-worthy, great cook, independent, affectionate, *really* funny.'

'She sounds lovely... but are you truly happy Fe?'

Felix looked at her, it was the second time she had asked him, was it unintentional repetition, especially in light of the list of qualities he had just reeled off. Or was it just because she was pissed? Was it out of genuine friendship or simple curiosity of an ex-lover?

'Yeah, course I am. It's never going to be like the first two years, when you count the minutes to be with each other–'

'Like we used to be.'

'Exactly, but the sex wears off after a bit, and if what you are left with makes you content and happy, then you think the next step is kids together, maybe marriage in between. We are both fortunate that we are realistic about life, grounded. Lucky that both sets

81

of grandparents want to look after the kids as well, gives us time together.'

'Where is she from, Abi?'

'Preston.'

'Always knew you would end up with a Northern lass.'

'It was not pre-ordained. It could have quite easily been you; you are the antithesis of *northern lass!'*

Charlotte swirled the champagne in her drink before she put it to her mouth, smiled and swallowed it.

'So you in for the long haul then, you think?'

'Nothing is definite, but I would be a fool to give up what we have, and the kids are a massive game changer.'

'The bairns.'

'Aye pet, the bairns like.'

'I suppose it is, maybe that's what killed dad, staying for the sake of me, knowing the option would be disastrous for me otherwise.'

'You turned out alright!'

Charlotte looked at him for a while, hesitated. She seemed to stop herself before she spiralled down into introspective self-analysis.

'Uhm, but now I feel that I have changed, and everything is going to be ok, better late than never. Might even get a translating job, get some routine in my life.'

'Might be interesting.'

'Yes, maybe.'

Charlotte swayed her drink in a circle and looked up from it at Felix, then back at her drink.

'Go on ask, you're going to anyway.'

Charlotte smiled. He knew her so well—at least he thought he did. If only he'd seen that last day in the garden coming. Things could have been so different now?

'Does Abi know you have come to meet me, did you tell her?'

'No.'

'Why didn't you tell her?'

'I didn't want her to feel jealous.'

'Would she have been jealous Felix?'

'Not sure. Maybe not, but if I knew then, what I know about you now, then maybe she may have felt threatened. People are bound to be a little threatened by previous boy-friends and girl-friends, because you had something special and intimate, a bond, a shared past, something that attracted you to each other. Especially... if it was a first proper love.'

'Is a shared bond, a way of saying love for each other?'

'It could be, but sometimes when you are young, you think it's love and it was something else, infatuation, sex, exciting new experience, a feeling of being a grown up...'

'And what did we have Felix?'

Felix thought for a moment. He did not need to. He had agonised over it enough to make an innate response.

'We had the real deal, yeah, if we could have grown together, wanted the same things, which back then we seemed to, we might have been holding hands walking into the sunset.'

'Do you think you ever stop fancying someone you loved?'

'It fades, probably disappears eventually, extinguishes itself with time. It must do. It depends on how the relationship finishes. If both end up hating each other and want to kill each other, then you are not going to still fancy them. You hear of a lot people, especially those that have had kids together, they sometimes become like brother and sister, maybe they have to for the sake of the children. Do they still fancy each other sexually? Probably not, but they probably still love each other in a different way, the way you love a friend.'

'First love is the big one though, you think?'

'Yeah, I think it is. A guy I used to work with went out with a girl in his sixth form in Birmingham. They split up when they went off to Uni. He stayed single, unmarried anyway. She went off to work in Singapore. She had kids, both teenagers, when the marriage split up. She came back to England with her two boys, and she tracked him down, via friends and the internet. She had come out of the marriage with a lot of money through a company she had set up out there and here, very wealthy. When they met up, they were just like teenagers again. It was refreshing; they should've been a bit jaded, but he said he looked at her and she was still eighteen. She would always be eighteen to him. He said he knew it sounded ridiculous, and he is a very erudite rational man, not subject to flights of fancy, but when you saw them together, they *were* teenagers once more, born again lovers. You had no doubt they had found each other, and I think he thought, that no one he ever met after her matched up. He met and had briefish relationships with lots of women. It's like a soldier or a pop star that dies when they are young; they are forever that age, *they shall not grow old.* Your first love is always that age, even though logically you know they have grown old. You can't picture them easily any other way, especially if you never see them again. You know you have grown old, you look in the mirror every morning and lines have appeared, grey hairs, but they are illogically out there still young and fresh faced, looking a million dollars.'

'*Wow,* you've thought that one through Felix?'

'I've looked in a lot of mirrors. That's the problem with my job, you have to think a lot of things through, to try and get some kind of end game, at least some sense to things. I remember it well. It was like a great love story. I was engrossed and excited for him. His exuberance was infectious. He became another person, and he would float into work on a Monday after meeting up with her. He gave you renewed hope about the world. Love does conquer all; a few of us in the office were re-living old romances through him. The food critic, who was a real gay curmudgeon, he couldn't wait to hear the next instalment. If *Gay C* could be infected, there was real hope for absolutely everyone.'

'So his love was a synecdoche thing?'

'Yes, I think it was, a utopian synecdoche, however anecdotal, yeah.'

'Are they still together?'

'*Oh God yes*, they are in for the long haul. They had another baby, until death do us part, without doubt. For them each other's arms is the only place in the world they want to be'

'Sounds lovely. *Love*, the most important of human conditions.' She sipped her wine and Felix waited to see if she was going to add something prophetic.

'It's like me and my ex.'

'*Which ex?*'

'She was called Julie Green. She was a researcher at ITV. When I came back from America, and started at *The Times*, we got together. It was good, but there was no massive passion, the same for both of us. I think we liked the idea of being in a relationship, the comfort of it, not having to be on the hunt all the time. We got on *really* well, the sex was ok. This sounds awful, but it felt like we were reinforcing the pair bond, more a comfort thing, lovely, but chemicals were not exploding. We were a bit old before our times' together. After two years we amicably said, it wasn't working, and we both agreed we would always remain friends, and we knew we meant it, which we always have. Abi and Julie get on really well. They're still close. When I see her I don't think about her in sexual way. I don't even think about what we did together, or what she looks like naked–not sure if that makes sense?'

'Uhm. Yeah, maybe'

'But when Julie and Abi are together, they say it's a tad weird when someone asks how they know each other? They always joke, but they are not embarrassed, they say things like, "We share lovers." "I break in lovers for Abi, so they are tame in the bedroom." "We mud wrestled for a man a long time ago and Julie won!" Or the one that always makes me laugh, Abi will say, "I won her in a raffle,' and Julie will reply, "I was second prize!" When anyone with a sense of humour asks what was first prize, they point at me and say together raucously, *"him."* While I laugh or look suitably embarrassed, and they giggle like school-girls.

Charlotte did not laugh, which Felix took for the effects of too much wine in the middle of the day.

'Has Julie met someone else?'

'Yeah, Jonathan, great bloke, freelance photographer and cameraman, out of the country a lot.'

'Kids?'

'One, Danny–slightly autistic, so it's hard work for them.'

86

'Must be hard if he's not around a lot of the time?'

'You make do; you have no other choice, do you? They often look exhausted, like they have been through sleep deprivation torture. Julie is battling with Danny some days and Jonathan is often exhausted from foreign assignments when he is back, often away in war zones. He's won a few big prizes, but it doesn't pay well, and you have to be bonkers to do it, but he does something he loves; it would worry me constantly, he's lost a few close friends and colleagues.'

'Sounds like scary shit to me?'

'And the rest probably. I once asked him why he didn't get a job in England, and he looked at me in all seriousness and said, "*It would fucking kill me!*" '
They both thought about this for a while. Felix finished his drink and placed it on the bar, even though there was still some champagne left in the bottle. He did not want to be so pissed that he fell asleep when he got in and the guilt he would associate to too much over-indulgence, when he should be helping out with the kids.

'I should think about getting off.'
Charlotte rubbed the top of his thigh. Felix liked it; it had been twelve years since he had allowed himself to like the close attention of a woman that was not his wife. The hairs bristled on the back of his neck and he felt a slight knotting of nerves and muscles in the front of his lower intestines.

'Don't go yet. I haven't seen you for fifteen years; please stay a little longer.' She carried on rubbing his thigh, imploring him with the up and down strokes of her palm. He knew she was drunk and he was well on the way. He thought there is no harm in

87

her touching him, two drunken friends; friends with a past that allowed harmless affection.

'Don't go, I want to talk to you longer Fe, I love talking to you. I miss talking to you.'

'I should, you know. Maybe we could meet with Trist?'

She pleaded more, 'Come up and see my room.' Felix tried to cut in but she spoke above him. 'Not for any you-know-what. Come and have a look at the room, it's absolutely amazing. Even I was impressed. If a hotel room can impress me, believe me, *it is* impressive.'

She could see Felix airing on the side of home and the comforts and safety it afforded.

'Twenty more minutes and that's it. *I promise.* Just have a look at the room, it's *absolutely* amazing.'

She could see the hesitation in his expression, but she was not sure what else to add.

'Ok, a quick gander. Twenty minutes only.'

Charlotte broke into a smile. She poured some of the champagne into their glasses, left some in the bottle and they both stood up together; mirroring each other. She saw a slight hesitancy in Felix's gaze and she readied herself to counter him if he had any further misgivings. They walked towards the door that led direct to the lifts. Charlotte, even through the haze of drunkenness, remembered to thread her large handbag through her left arm, as they reached the doors she excused herself and rushed back to the bar. Felix watched her exchange a few words with the barman, and he nodded his head in agreement. Felix waited by the lift, when it arrived he was surprised to see an attendant appear. They both watched her traverse the short distance, confident, her gaze fixed only on Felix, she smiled a thin smile at him and then informed the attendant, 'floor four'. They all fell silent in the lift. Felix sat on the embroidered padded bench and Charlotte looked down on him and smiled. They both tried not to stare at the attendant. Felix thought he was dressed like a Victorian monkey in a bar. How ridiculous he looked in the twenty-first century. Uncertain if the silence was due to 'lift syndrome,' or the fact he knew what he was doing might be a little reckless, he was not sure how he had come to agree to go back to Charlotte's room fifteen years after he last saw her, seventeen years since she had, *'quit'* him. He was turning back the clock to when everything with Charlotte and the world inside and outside Lady Margaret's was possible; he knew he was returning to his youth, the endless possibilities of his youth. There was something in Charlotte that drew men into her, something that had drawn him in all those years ago. He knew in the danger of the shut door; he had far more to lose. For him, this was bordering on madness; this was sailing away from the safety of the land. His train of thought however discordant, however fast it was flowing was awoken by the *ding* of the lift reaching the fourth floor. The sound greeted by Charlotte's smile first towards the attendant and then Felix. She stepped out and waited for him to follow suit.

'This way,' and she gestured at the same time. Felix watched her walking from behind. He was watching the rhythmic sway of her arse in her dress. She was aware of it and she liked it. She was guiding him; she was more in control now. He thought to himself. 'Why would you possibly have your arse augmented, when you already had a great one anyway?' He wondered if she had perfected the walk to look sexier, or she had always walked that way, he could not quite remember. She stopped outside the room and fished in her bag for her card-key. As she pulled it out she turned to Felix.

'Are you ready?'

Felix was not sure if there was duplicity in her tone; he thought there was. She handed her champagne glass to him without speaking and slid the card through the swipe, a little red LED light illuminated green, then faded. She pushed the door open by extending her backside and placed her foot at the bottom, then a little more, just enough to wrestle her handbag around. She let it fall to the ground inside.

'Right, come here and close your eyes.' Felix walked towards her and stopped at the door, she kept her backside against the door so it would not swing shut and placed her hands over Felix's eyes. They felt slender and warm, massaging his eyes below. Awkwardly they shuffled around; like two fat people waltzing in high heels, after too much to drink.

'No peeping, until I say.'

'Ok.' Felix replied with contrition, but excited at the same time. He knew for Charlotte to be excited by opulence, it had to be something special.

'Bit further–try not to step on the servants, just a bit further, right.' She removed her hands from his face and stood back against the wall. Felix still had his eyes closed, like a compliant small child.

'You can open them now.'

She saw Felix's eyes widen in a sheer amazement. He expected to find a bed in the middle of the room against a wall, table, wardrobe and a small en suite bathroom off to the side; he had not given it enough thought. He had not visualised the room. What he found instead was not the mundane, but an exquisite art deco drawing room, at the centre of which was an enormous glass topped table with wrought-iron filigree legs, in a sweeping cursive art deco style with two armchairs and a two-seater settee, a large black and white checked material inlayed into the centre of all three, all faced a flat screen tv housed in a wooden walnut cabinet in one corner. There was an embossed pattern to match the furniture; the pattern reminded him of the Chrysler Building. Against one of the walls was a deco drinks cabinet sectioned into three, in the middle section were two glass sliding panels, containing many different but matching glasses and a silvered cocktail shaker. One end he assumed housed a concealed fridge. What was at the other end, he was not sure. Care had been taken to match the furniture. Silver decorative mirrors and 1930's film posters in frames adorned the walls. One large floor to ceiling window, in front of which was a long red settee, that reminded him of the one she had back in her room at college, but bigger. Two bulky rectangular arms at either end jutted out; its colour seemed incongruous in comparison to its immediate monochrome surroundings. He walked over to the glass-topped table, thick glossy magazines arranged like fallen dominoes, a bottle of perfume, an old-fashioned letter writing set, next to which, a hand written note of welcome, with a fountain pen in a beautiful curlicue calligraphic style. He picked it up to inspect it: *Dear Ms Covington, Welcome to Claridge's. We hope you will enjoy your stay. Do not hesitate to ask if you need any assistance. Kind regards Victor Krumm, Hotel Manager.*

She had been studying him, patient. She could see he was impressed with the room.

'Very posh, pet. Like stepping back in time." He held the welcome card up to her.

'The little touches Fe.'

'This room *is* incredible.'

91

'Come and look at the bedroom.' Charlotte grabbed Felix by the hand, and led him through the room. She let her fingers drape over the arm of the red settee as she passed. He felt like he was in a lavish palace, being led through somewhere amazing he had not encountered before. She stood next to the enormous bed, still with his hand in hers. Their knees butted against the soft opulence. She turned to him without smiling, and whispered, 'What do you think, Fe?'

He tried to work out once more if there was duplicity in her words. Whether they were deliberate, calculated, drunken or otherwise, or was he reading too much into them?

'So far it's amazing.' He turned to look at the wardrobes, let his fingers drip from hers. He walked over to them, felt their polished varnish with his right palm. The full-length walnut wardrobes filled the whole of one side of the room nearest the door, a spraying carved fountain of wood sprung from the centre. Charlotte opened the middle two of the eight doors and stood back a little. Felix moved over for a closer inspection. They went back twice as far as he expected, twice as far as the ones in his own home. One side had chunky wooden coat hangers and the adjacent side was sectioned into compartments of varying sizes. Each had a small white enamelled inlay bound by chrome edging; he read four of the smaller ones just below eye level: 'handkerchiefs' 'socks' 'cufflinks' 'cravats.'

Charlotte flopped onto the bed and sank her head into the multitude of pillows stacked up against the headboard. She watched Felix inspecting the wardrobe in more detail. The two side tables each had reproduction period clock/radios, lamp, a cut crystal glass and telephone.

92

'Impressed?'

'Very much so, very extravagant.'

She threw one of the pillows at Felix. 'How many bloody pillows do people need? You end up putting most of them on the floor at night.'

Felix ignored her. 'What's the bathroom like?'

'Incredible,' she said trying to sound casual. 'Come on, I'll show you.' She wrestled herself from the bed and walked over to the door and held her hand out for him, he took it. She led him across the drawing room and into the bathroom. She kept hold of his hand once inside.

'Oh wow, this is incredible Charlie.'

At the far end of the large room was a free standing shower unit that could not only power wash you, but massage you at the same time. Two matching sinks in white heavy marble with flames of electric blue tanzanite naturally feathered through them.

'Look at the bath, Fe.' Charlotte dragged him over to it and stroked the inside. Felix followed suit with his free hand, smooth and cold. A free standing enamelled bath with Victorian taps and shower attachment in the middle, big enough for two tall people. The bath was situated against a translucent floor to ceiling square glass panelled window. Felix leaned over to read the words on two circular enamelled buttons with silver outlay: maid and valet. He turned to face her; he could not disguise his amazement. She looked deep into him and it checked him. She felt like their breathing was in synchrony, she dragged her index finger slowly once across his palm, he was uncertain if it was involuntary. They both looked down at their clasped hands as the drifting digit came to rest. Then their stares locked again. She looked deep within him and held the gaze. Neither of them smiled now. A calm descended and the sound of

93

a vehicle horn entered the room. Felix looked over to the window above the bath. His hand left her grip and he pointed with the same hand at the round servants' calling buttons.

'Do they work?' Charlotte did not answer him immediately, so he reiterated. 'What do you think?'

'Why wouldn't they? This is Claridge's, darling.' She replied quietly.

He stood up prone and looked down on the bath. 'That's amazing isn't it?'

'It certainly is.' She agreed more brightly.

'Incredible. Have you had a go yet?'

'No, not yet, I only got the room an hour before I met you. If you want a bath, there are enough towels to dry a football team, robes, slippers.' She grazed her hand over the fluffy towels and robes hung on silver pegs on the wall.

'Tempting.'

He watched her kick her shoes off and slide her feet into the soft white footwear. Her tights appeared to make them slide in smoother.

'Come on, let's go and sit down.' Charlotte went over to the large settee, grabbing their drinks on the way and rested against one arm, kicking off the loose fitting slippers. She stretched her legs across it and sipped on her champagne. Felix sat at the other end with his legs dangling down. 'I never thought this would happen again, after what I did to you.' Felix looked at her but did not say anything. 'I'm sorry for what I did to you. I do regret it bitterly Felix, you do believe me, don't you?'

Felix considered it for a moment. He did believe her, but he had never truly worked out why you would destroy something so special, something so harmonious.

'I still don't fully understand why you walked away Charlie. Nothing was broken?'

She looked at her feet and thought about it for a while, he waited for an answer; the answer he had waited for all those years ago and never received, when he needed it most. When it had tormented him, and no amount of passing time, logic or reasoning brought out any more clarity to the event. She moved her gaze to her champagne glass and swivelled it carefully in her fingers.

'I was an idiot Felix, insecure. I thought I would end up like my mother and I would do to you what she did to my dad. I thought somewhere down the line I would look at you, us, and I would have known that her legacy was your unhappiness.' Charlotte started to well with emotion. Felix stretched an arm out and rubbed her feet; that had now withdrawn farther towards her body.

'Why did you not tell me this seventeen years ago Charlie?'

She looked vulnerable, maybe that was the legacy of her mother coming out.

'I knew if I had, you would have convinced me that everything would be ok, but I couldn't see how it could be. I saw my mother destroy my father, a successful intelligent happy man, *drip, drip*, through a process of osmosis and passive-aggressive torture. I was not even sure if it was intentional, but she did, and I thought I would do that to you. I couldn't have that on my conscience. I didn't feel that I could take the risk. Did you see her the day we were distraught in the car park at College—not a flicker of emotion, the ice-maiden. Her only daughter leaving the only man she'd *ever truly* loved, and not a flicker... They say look at the mother, and–'

'But you have not turned out like your mother?'

'No, not as bad, *no*, but I have destroyed good men, left them in my wake. It has taken the passing of the years for me to realise we would have made it, realise I'm not the same as my mother. I'm not my mother's keeper. Only time could give me the answer to the ultimate question, but time is the one thing you *can never* claw back, *time…*' She tapered off.

'You cannot compare yourself to your mother.'

'It took me a long time to work out what was wrong with her. When I say a long time, I only worked it out a few years after dad died. What do you think is wrong with her Felix?'

'I think she has Autism, but it has never been diagnosed properly.'

'That's probably one of the many things she has. I have read lots about it. She has borderline personality disorder, probably plural disorders. That's why she cannot empathise with people properly. Look at our last day–most mothers would have banged our heads together and said, 'stop this bloody madness, you love each other, this is as good as it gets, *you lucky bastards!* You don't know how good you have it."'

'Probably, yes.' Felix felt the clenched gloom of that day envelop him once more, throw its damp cloak over him. If his mother or father, or both were there that day, things would have been different; their history book would be very different, their books would never have diverged, only to converge seventeen years later. If Charlotte's dad had been there also, she would have listened to him. If he had told her she was possessed, but she would be exorcised, Felix would cleanse her, make her whole, and it would pass. She would have believed him; he would have exorcised the doubts away like ignited alcohol, they would have spun and danced away to leave no trace, no suspicion or hesitation ever again for her. Words that would march on even after his death, words that would weld them together in times of doubt, like the words of Saint Mandela all those years ago.

'Unfortunately I have made mistakes that I cannot undo. And it has taken me far too long to realise, I'm more my father's child than my mother's. But her disease has tainted me. She is like a recurrent malaria. You can be well with it most of your life, but when the malaise descends on you, it masks rationality, the parasites take control.'

Felix listened to the words she had mulled over endlessly, tortured herself with, her Spanish Inquisition. She smiled at Felix.

'What is your earliest memory Felix?'

'Bamburgh Castle. I was three–the whole family were there and we rounded the dunes on to the beach and I saw it in the near distance. I can remember the thrill now. It was so splendid, so solid and magnificent. I ran on, I couldn't wait to touch it, get inside, dispel any marauders...' She smiled at him, excited at the thought, her smile dropped away.

'My first memory was being used as a mop when I accidentally weed on the floor when I was about three. My mother was so angry with me, she literally wiped the floor with me. I did not realise that was not normal behaviour–how could you at that age.' Felix chose to let her carry on. 'When I first realised how manipulative she was, I would have been about five. I heard my mum and dad having a fierce argument. My dad didn't really do arguing. He was passive–anything for an easy life. He shouted at her. "I will not allow you to drive a wedge between us, so you can then step in and take control." That was the first time I realised maybe she was not like all the other

97

mums.' She shot back in time, the face muscles below her skin contorted with anguish.

'Can you forgive her Charlie?'

Children always forgave their parents when they were wronged by them, especially with the benefit of life, the realisation they were just mere mortals, Felix speculated.

'No! I can understand her more now. But I cannot forgive her, not for what she did to my father. I know maybe I should, but she would never get help now. She is beyond help. If you are not prepared to accept help, admit there is a problem, you can never move forward. I know you will not truly understand that Fe, because you come from such a wonderful family. Your family dished out love freely like sweets. I know it makes me sound callous and empty. I just try and shut her out, it's my coping mechanism; however flawed. I know for a child to reject their own parent sounds despicable, but I feel she rejected me years ago...' She hesitated, her voice heavy with resentment, '...She never replaced us with anything else... anything better.'

'I understand. I have met her lots of times.' He did not fully understand, but there was little mileage in expressing his doubts.

'That's why it's so good to talk to you Felix. I feel that you will not judge me, like a lot of people would. You have met her, and you understand what she's like, and when she met you, she was on her very best behaviour; that was as good as she got.'

'I think it's sad though Charlie.'

'That's because it is sad Fe, it's beyond sad. To be in London, and *not want* to visit your own mother—loathe the thought of meeting your own mother; when she is only an hour away. It's not just sad, it is *completely fucked up!'*

Felix tried to imagine it, but he found the concept very difficult to envisage. Charlotte had always said her mother was on her best behaviour when Felix ever visited. Charlotte watched him thinking about it. She knew she was quite unique, but not in a good way. Felix muttered a noise to indicate he had at least heard what she was saying.

'What saved me was boarding school. I was eight when I went. Some of the other homesick girls used to cry at night. But I knew school was my salvation. I have heard some people, people I know well, say that boarding makes you less emotionally intelligent, less empathetic, having to strive to pass exams and get well paid jobs in a need to please your parents. They felt rejected by their parents, being packed off to be looked after by people they didn't know... School didn't do that to me, she did. School saved me Fe! However cold people say boarding is, it was never as cold as her.'

He nodded his head attentively.

'I wish I was wiser. I wish, Fe, I had shared my thoughts with you, but I still might have hurt you measurably. I might have burdened you, weighed you down with my load... Will you do me a favour Felix?'

Felix was not sure what was coming. Before he could say, 'it has to depend on what *it* is?' Charlotte continued.

'Would you take your shoes off and put your feet next to mine, like we used to do on the big red settee in my room all those years ago?'

Felix did not reply; he undid his shoe laces and placed the palms of his feet adjacent to Charlottes'. He started to curl his toes around and between hers; they shimmied and danced against each other. Charlotte shut her eyes and leaned her head back against the arm. Felix moved his big toes into the balls of her feet

99

and pressed them hard, massaged them. His smaller toes ran over her smaller toes. He curled the out-step of his feet into the edge of her instep, probing into the muscles, reaching into them. He knew for them it was the same as a French kiss, a rub of noses. It was fore-play; half seduction, half total relaxation. He knew what it felt like; hundreds of times their feet had tangled in a courtship dance. He remembered how she sometimes pleaded with him to massage her feet with his, especially after she had been wearing '*ridiculous shoes*,' as he called high heels back then. It was the settee in her room in Lady Margaret's that informed him that they could spend the rest of their lives together. It was the *foot-sex*, as they called it, that told them both that *if*, which in those days was very unlikely, *if* the sex waxed and waned, it could never wane–*surely?* But if it did, the *foot-sex* told them that everything would be fine. It was the *foot-sex* that told them whatever was happening outside in the world, it did not matter because they had each other. He looked at Charlotte, her lips and closed eyes moving with diminutive twisted happiness, mirroring the movements of his toes. He looked into the gap of seventeen years, into the drifting void of what-might-have-been; looked at the dissipated years, the years that had not seemed to age her.

'Sorry, I was miles away,' she said without opening her eyes, almost purring like a cat.

'Your room in Oxford?'

'Yes, with a young under-graduate that I was in love with. This is a moment that I thought could never happen again.' She uttered with a susurrus lilting in her tone. 'And I know I'm pissed, but it feels so right, both physically and emotionally. I feel as though you have forgiven me. If you have not, please don't spoil the moment Fe, just let me drift in a sea of contentment a while.'

Felix thought she had found some form of contentment. He decided to reciprocate her honesty; he reached back into the past. Now was the time.

'I was in New York, a few months after we had parted. *Hitch*, Christopher Hitchens, was hosting a night at one of the rooms in the Carnegie. The series of talks were entitled: *'Forgiveness: the Moral High Ground.'* A load of Second World War vets were giving talks about their experiences in the war. Two he had interviewed for an article written for the *New Yorker*. So he knew what two of them were going to talk about in some detail, he'd implored me to come. I remember the words he said to me in the office, *'Sometimes Felix, men have to cry because it's right, and sorrow is the only option, the last option. Sometime history can only be reinforced if men cry in public together. When men cry in public, great change comes about.'* So I knew what was coming, I was supposed to be meeting Libby, my then girlfriend that night. So I convinced her to come, instead of the pictures, knowing it would be harrowing. *God they were harrowing talks*, from men that might have been doing it for the last time, summoning up enough courage and energy for one last push. One Jewish guy, Goodman, a Dutch immigrate after the war, talked about putting his wife and daughter on the back of a truck in Holland. They were transported to separate concentration camps; he naively told how he would find them after the war, as the Nazis shipped them to Auschwitz, while he went to Buchenau. I have never seen a whole room of adults, *and I mean everyone*, maybe two hundred people, cry as one. Then an American came on that was captured in the Far-East and sent to build the railway in Burma. He was a big bloke, six-three. He was an amateur boxer before the war, just about to turn pro when America joined and he was conscripted. He weighed sixteen stone, by the end of the war he weighed just a little over seven. He talked about burying the dead. It was his job to dig the graves and bury the dead; he buried hundreds. At one point he was so hungry he ate the rotting leather off his shoes. He built to this point about his friends dying and how inhumanely the Japanese guards had treated them all, they rammed a wooden pole into his mid-riff and broke three of his ribs for no apparent reason, they still made him work, he showed us the indent where the ribs had healed inwards and crooked.'

Charlotte opened her eyes to look at him. Felix was staring at her.

'He said one day he couldn't take it anymore; they had not just broken him, they'd taken away his will to live, left him desperate to die, pleased to die, next to his friends. He could see no end to the war, and if it did come he was so humiliated that he felt he could never face his family. He'd climbed in the grave next to the dead and said to his friend, *"bury me alive with them, please, just cover me up, I can't take it anymore!"* He pleaded with his friend to bury him. At this point my mind flew off from him and the story, and I thought I knew what he meant. I knew what it was like to have no hope, only escape from the pain. That was me in the car park and the weeks that followed, after you left me.'

The tears trickled down Charlotte's face. Felix held his back. She pushed her feet away from him and withdrew, wrapped her arms around her knees. She forced the words out.

'*I am so sorry,* believe me... *please.*'

She could see the tears welling in his eyes, trying to hold them back. They looked at each other like

102

children. Like no one had equipped them for days like these. He wiped his teetering tears before they fell with his suit cuff.

'*I do*... Why did you not just speak to me about your doubts Charlie? We would have sorted it.'

'*I am soo* sorry, it was a mistake... I was confused, I was young.' She was still oscillating with emotion. 'The spectre of my mother always watched over me, haunted me. If I'd known I was not cursed–at least not fully cursed anyway, if I thought you could have fixed me, guided me. Do you think I would have walked away from *yo?* You were my world. You were the happiness I thought I would never ever find, but I didn't think I deserved to destroy *your* happiness... I felt I did not have the right to do that. A right to you.'
They both stopped and observed each other, then composed themselves.

'It does not make any sense Charlie?' Felix was half pleading with her. She shook her head from side to side before she answered.

'Of course it doesn't. There was no sense to be made of it back then, not by me anyway. But now, it all makes sense. If I'd told you, it's so easy to say now, you would have helped me, fixed me, held me in your arms and reassured me; had foot-sex with me, loved me unconditionally, but I wouldn't let you in to heal me Felix, not then. I couldn't take the risk with you. It has worked out better for you. You have the nice life, the nice wife, the nice children... I don't mean *nice* in a nasty way, Fe.'

'In what way?'

'In a jealous way, Fe. It could have been you and me and the kids. If I was not so messed up back then–look at what I've achieved with my life, look what I've thrown away...'

'What have you thrown away Charlie?'

She looked at him, the intense serious stare that he knew from all those years ago.

'I threw away you, then Steven, and a chance at happiness, for what? For the chance to make loads of money, and feel desired by lots of men, who then discarded me and placated their guilt by lavishing presents and money on me. The home, the kids, the career, the contentment, the kudos, all the things I didn't want, are all the things I'm yearning for now. But I'm playing catch-up.'

Felix let her vent her remorse; something she must have agonised and pored over. 'I heard that Eagles' song, about having lots of money but not enough time. That's me now Felix. It shouldn't be; it's not as though you, then Steven would have not loved me until our dying breaths. *Us*, that is my regret–what I have to live with. I cannot expect anyone to feel any great sympathy towards me, why should they? I have made my expensive bed, now I have to lie in it alone, at least for a while longer, hopefully not forever. Forever is a long time.' She was about to continue, when there was a knock on the door. She unfolded herself and walked across the room, and opened it, surprised to see a fresh faced young man with a freestanding champagne cooler resting under his arm.

'Your champagne.'

'Can you bring it over to the settee?, thanks.'

'Certainly.'

He lumbered the wine cooler over to the side of the settee, the rhythmic clink of ice against the side of the cooler. Felix smiled at him and the young man returned it. They both watched in silence as he strode across the room and obtained two elegant champagne flutes from the cabinet.

'That's fine, you can leave the glasses on the side.' She was a little annoyed that the interruption had stopped the flow of their conversation, but she tried not to let it show. She stood holding a note loosely in her hand.

'Is there anything else you need?' Enquired the smartly dressed youth.

'No thank you.'

'Enjoy your champagne.'

She proffered the note to him. His eyes lit up when he saw its actual denomination.

'Thank you very much.'

She shut the door behind him, grabbed the two flutes off the side and went and sat back in her original position.

'I think I'm pissed Felix?'

'You were pissed a long time ago. It has just caught up with you now, press-ganged you.' They both smiled at each other. She put the glasses on the floor.

'Massage my feet again.'

'Ok, but I'm not drinking anymore.'

'I'm sick of champagne now. It does get a rather dry after a while, do you not think?'

'After the second Magnum, yeah.'

'I've had far too much haven't I?'

'Not sure how much you drink in the middle of the afternoon, normally?'

'Shall I get some water for us both? We don't have to pretend we are nineteen again. That's the sensible thing. Look after me Felix.'

'I'll get it.'

He went over to where he assumed the drinks would be in the cabinet. He was correct; there was a concealed fridge behind the wooden panel door. He poured two mini green bottles of sparkling water, and noticed the thistle on the side as he did so; the water came half the way up the ornate glasses. He remembered when Trist, Charlotte and he had gone up to Aviemore to ski just after New Year, in the holiday. Only Charlotte could ski, not that there was much snow; only on the highest ground, compacted ice mainly. Trist had half given up on the dry slope even before he had put his skis on. Then when he endeavoured, he was horrified to find himself and Felix in a beginner's class of mainly primary school children. *"We are like a couple of fucking giants, Gulliver and his bigger brother."* They spent the entire week-end getting pissed.

Felix returned with the water and passed one down to Charlotte on the settee. He wanted to steer the conversation away from them, the split, the remorse, the pain. He felt they had said enough now.

'Do you remember that time we went up to Aviemore to try and ski and we spent the entire weekend getting pissed?'

'Oh God yes. Best skiing holiday I ever had. Trist was so funny. Remember, he went out to get some vodka and he came back with that terrible landscape painting from the charity shop.'

'And we both looked at him perplexed and asked. "Do you like it Trist, I wouldn't have thought it was your cup of Tequila?"'

Charlotte laughed before she recalled it. *"No, it's fucking awful, but it will remind me of you two lovers, and us."* He used to call us lovers, remember?'

'Or *shaggers*, or *fornicators*, or *beasts of the field*, or *adulterers*, or *perverts.*'

'What was that mad made up one he said when he was really drunk, began with a 'q'?'

'*Quibblers.*'

'That's it *quibblers.* He always said it was from Shakespeare, didn't he.'

106

Felix sat back down at the far end of the settee and they placed their feet against each other's once more. Charlotte started to massage his feet this time. They were transported back again. Felix closed his eyes and Charlotte regarded him. She was back in the room with him again. She felt like she had been freed once more–released from captivity, free to fly wherever she wanted to. But she had flown to too many places. She felt she was a bird with no legs; she could land, always clumsy, never easy. Enough of flying now–she wanted to settle, but she was like a wandering albatross. She knew so many places, but so few people there. Now she wanted the sanctuary of a roost. Now she wanted to nest, like the Royal Albatrosses of Dunedin. That is where she had come up with her theory of herself as a bird with no legs–*tout autour de toi, vite, vite.* While the tour guide waffled on about the details of the woeful gun emplacement, situated near their nests–supposedly to dispel the Japanese in the Second World War. She had left behind the images of the approaching Japanese Admirals. Flying yet again, this time with Albatrosses on the wing, searching, but for what, at that point she was not sure.

She concentrated on rubbing the inside edges of his feet, in deep with the balls of hers; like he used to love; especially after he had played football. Felix had shut his eyes; she knew the two places where his body was, but not his mind. She guessed it would not be thousands of miles away on the wing of an albatross. He had never wandered far from home, never felt the need to. He had nothing to escape, nothing to run from. Home was England; home was where the heart and the love had always been and always would be. That she envied, that is what she missed, being happy in your own skin, happy in your own home, happy to wander in your own land contented, always discovering something new in the familiar.

'Do you think I'm ok Fe?'
Felix was jolted back from Oxford, transported from one room of privilege to another.

'What do you mean?' He said relaxed, as though being awoken by a masseur.

'Do you think I will be ok?'

'Are you not ok now? You seem ok to me. You seem together. It was bound to be a little emotional today, after what we had and lost. You seem to have learned the lessons you need to move on successfully, happily.'

'I suppose that answers my question.'

'Are you not ok?' Felix enquired with more concern.

'Yes. I'm fine, but with you, I'm bound to feel–'

'We are friends now, good friends. Everything's sorted.'

'Good friends that have not seen each other for fifteen years.'

'We are having foot-sex. I only have *foot-sex* with *very good friends*.'
Charlotte smiled at Felix.

'You are lovely Fe. I was a young fool to let you go.'

'Let's not go there again, water-under-the-bridge.'

'You still have not told me if you have forgiven me or not.'
Felix spluttered out laughter.

'After *foot-sex*.' Charlotte laughed back at him. At the same time it made her sad. She felt guilty because he was wonderful and she had discarded him like a one night stand. When he had stood naked for

108

her, taken off his armour for her, when he could give no more, she had pierced his soft flesh and walked away and left him wounded on the battlefield, and not returned to nurse him, even check on him.

'You will be fine. You will find someone new to have *foot-sex* with. A new *foot-sexinator.*' He put on an Arnold Schwarzenegger voice, 'sent back through time.'

She fixed him with spellbound eyes. It was a stare he was uncertain of.

'*What?*'

'What if I don't meet someone?'

'Of course you will, look at you, you're attractive, witty, very intelligent and good company. You're just having doubts, a little wobble, that's natural, human nature.'

'I hope you're right Fe. I hope–'

'I need the toilet. Then I will have to think about making a move.'

'So we are *really, really good friends* again, *yes?*'

'Of course we are. I have to have a pee.'

Felix got up and wandered over to the bathroom. He sat to urinate, as he had felt his phone vibrate a couple of times in his pocket. There were two text messages. The first was from Trist: 'How did you get on with Charlie?' He had done well to remember he was meeting her, he thought to himself. He thought about what to text back, or whether he should just leave it until he was on the underground later, or even ring him then. He decided on: 'Just about to leave, has been nice catching up.' The other was from Abi: 'What time you home? Will you be back for tea?' It was a nudge back to the present, a nudge back to his life of contentment. He texted back: 'One hour.' He stared at the grand bath, he noticed, as he got up to wash his

109

hands, he had left the door ajar by about ten centimetres. He chose the smallest towel, from the plethora of towels that were on offer.

He noticed Charlotte as soon as he left the bathroom. It was the change in contrast from black on red, to flesh on red; that registered first, before he focused on her in more shocked detail. She had taken her dress off and was laid out with just a black push-up lacy bra, matching stockings and garter belt on. She was wearing no knickers and a strip of pubic hair two centimetres wide in a perfect vertical symmetry, like a landing strip was left, at the top of the ribbon of hair was a piercing, a diamond sparkled diffracted light. The disbelief had taken his breath away; uncertain whether to just walk straight out, or walk to the main door and speak from there, then leave. Shock turned to instant anger.

'What are you doing Charlotte?'

'I have slipped into something more comfortable for you.'

'No, no, Charlotte.' He gave a violent shake of his head from side to side. 'Put your dress back on *now.'*

'Don't be a prude, Fe. Come and sit with me, touch me.'

'For fuck sake Charlotte, what are you doing?'

'Marcus Aurelius said that conscience is acting within the limits of reason. Why don't we let our reason find some common ground?'

'For fuck's sake Charlie! If you don't put your dress back on, I'm gone.'

She knew he was not joking. She tried to think of a time when he had had such forcefulness in his voice, apart from a political debate. She knew she had over-stepped the mark. Read the situation wrong– *'really, really, good friends'* –made a fool of herself. She got

110

up and turned her back to him. He looked away from her as she slipped her dress back on, something within him wanted to look at her arse, see if it had changed–could he recollect what it was like all those year ago anyway? He was looking away from her when she turned to face him. She was flushed with embarrassment. She moved towards him, he sensed her movement and turned to her. He could see she was mortified, but he was still angry.

'I am so sorry Felix. I thought that you know… For old time's sake.'

'What gave you that impression, for *Christ's sake*?'

'The *foot-sex*. We always made love after *foot-sex*.'

She could sense the tensed controlled anger still in his voice as he reminded her.

'That was seventeen years ago… When we were going out.'

'I'm so sorry Felix. Please forgive me.'

She blushed further as she neared him. They stood opposite each other–they did not speak. He watched her like a hidden hunter watched his prey, waiting to work out her next move; still flushed with embarrassment. Felix felt like he was a rich punter with a high end prostitute, whatever he asked for she would have to oblige.

'I'm sorry for shouting at you, but, you know, it was a bit of a shock to see you like that.'

'Sorry, honest.' He could see she was really embarrassed, mortified.

'Right, let's sit down and talk about this.'

'Yeah, right, ok.'

They sat back at opposite ends of the settee, with their legs on the floor and turned to face each other.

111

'Sorry. I was having such a lovely time with you. I thought you might have wanted to, you know?'

'No.'

'Had the thought not crossed your mind at all?'

'Maybe a little, when we were having foot-sex, but I didn't want to have full sex.'

'Sorry, I have over-stepped the mark. I have spoilt it, spoilt the afternoon, haven't I?'

'It was just a shock that's all. You go for a piss and your ex-girlfriend is laid out on a plate.'

'Sorry.'

'Why do you want to have sex with me now, after all these years?'

'Nostalgia, I wanted to go back to that room in Oxford. I wanted to go back to what we had. It was so great back then. I got greedy and I wanted to know if it would be the same.'

'How could it be the same Charlie?'

'You're right, but I got carried away. I'm sorry Felix–Far too much wine.'

'No harm done. And with a body like that you will not have many problems getting a man.' Charlotte smiled at him, she knew he was being kind and letting her off the hook. When a lot of men with Felix's moral code would have walked away.

'Can we rewind to before I made a fool of myself Fe?'

'We can. Is there something you are not telling me Charlie?'

'Like what?'

'I don't know. Something bigger?'

'Don't think so… No.'

She knew now was not the best time to ask, but she knew time was running out. She had miscalculated, read the signals wrong, made a complete fool of herself; she could live with that. She wondered if now

112

he would avoid another meeting with her, even with Trist there. She was compelled to ask, she had to know.

'Will you tell Abi that you have met me today?' Felix thought before he spoke. Meta-cognition, as his father would always say to him and his brother when they were growing up – "*Thinking time is the most important time there is.*"

'Probably, yes.'

'*Really?*' Charlotte was incredulous. She inhabited a clandestine world, where the people she knew would never go home and tell their wives–insane with jealousy–never worth the hassle.

'Why would I not? I won't tell her about you on the settee about to distribute free love. I may have to be *a little* economical.'

'That's slightly reassuring, at least.'

'But if you and I and Trist are going to go out for a drink, or rip it up like the old days. What is the point of lying to her?' Charlotte was a little confused and it showed on her face. 'Would you not want your husband to tell you if he was meeting with an ex-girlfriend?'

Charlotte thought about it, and thought about the economy of truth. There was no point about lying now, not now she had been quite honest with him.

'I think I would be jealous, Fe.'

'Yeah, you might be, but you would be glad he told you. Glad because you knew you could trust him and respect him for telling you. Then after your insecurity had settled down, you would love him more, because you would know she was not a threat.'

'So I'm not a threat then?'

'Not anymore no, sixteen, fifteen years ago maybe, it may have been different, but I cannot give up what I have now. I cannot leave my children. Don't

113

get me wrong, if we were both single, things would be different. *Foot-sex* wouldn't have been enough. But things change, you have to put your family first. Seeing you today Charlie has opened a can of worms for me…'

'And me.'

'We had two fantastic years together. You are friends with one of my best friends. It would be a shame to deny the past happened. I often think, definitely used to think a lot, that I wished that it could have all been different. I believed we would have been happy together. But I had to let go of you. I had to stop hating you for what you did to me. If you let your hatred get the better of you, it can consume you and imprison you. That's not healthy at all. About a year after we had finished, Arran came down; we went clubbing, a few of us. Arran had brought some drugs, he was banging on about how good they were, how they were the *dog's bollocks*. I don't know what was in them, real lovey ones, but, Trist was there and we were talking about you. Arran had been off dancing, he'd just had his first child; he was over the moon to be a dad, radiant. Trist explained to him what we were talking about. He came up to me, cupped me in his hands, ephemerally, he spoke lightly, but assertive, *"Listen Felix, listen carefully to what I'm about to say to you. Remember it for the rest of your life. She's gone–she will want you back, but you can't have her back, because she's damaged you. Let her go, she had her chance, but she left you wasted and broken. Never go back to her, even if she calls to you from the rocks. She had her chance and she blew it. You are Felix Fletcher-Boyd, Oxford graduate; the world is at your feet. I love you like a brother, but I will not let her haunt you anymore. Do you understand?'* The tears were falling down my eyes Charlie, but he exorcised

114

you from me. The tears were falling from Trist's eyes, he carried on, *"She's gone, where is she, tell me where she is?" "She's gone." "Where is she?" "She's gone."* And in that moment, aided by chemicals, I realised you *had gone*, and that night I forgave you, because I had to, because without forgiveness we are little more than murderers and prison guards.'

Charlotte rolled her shoulders, could keep her tears in no longer. She stood up and tried hard to force words out. She stood vibrating, ululating with emotion. Felix got up and pulled her in close and she rolled and contorted in his arms. She tried to break free, but he would not let her. She was hot with sorrow. She cleaved herself from him and ran to the bathroom. She did not return for about ten minutes. When she did he was stood equidistant between the door and the settee. She knew he was leaving. She knew no words from her could keep him any longer. Nearly all that needed saying had been said.

'An electrician from *NEW-caastle*... and a best friend, healed me, removed the last barrier, took away the final hurdle for me to move on. Would you credit that? ... An electrician from *NEW-caastle*! The World has changed Charlie, for better or for worse. It changes anyway, regardless. You will find someone. I think you are healed now. I hope you are.'

Charlotte just looked at him, uncertain what to say. It had not been as she had imagined; it had been more of a rollercoaster. She had made a fool of herself– embarrassment had been replaced by something else. She felt sad, a slight hollowing. Sad because he was leaving her now, and she would be alone.

'I will come with you to the door.'

'You don't need to. Do you want people to see you this upset?'

115

'I don't care. I would like to see you to the main entrance, if you would allow me to?'

'Course, come on then.'

She picked up her handbag. They never spoke once in the lift. The attendant looked at them, a knowing surreptitious look–they'd had a lover's tiff. It would work itself out in the fullness of time, he would forgive her, whatever she'd done. He would get over it; he could see it in his stance. They walked in silence through the foyer, through a collection of visiting Chinese, avoiding the main rotating doorway and stood to one side of the main entrance on the street, away from the two attendants, who looked like ushers at a wedding. Five flags on jutting poles fluttered above them in the wind: British, USA, Euro, Irish and Chinese Republic.

'Ok Fe, I am sorry for putting you in an awkward position… just sorry, sorry for lots of things… I'm a bit pissed, and I have had such a fantastic time with you again. I know I've made a fool of myself. Hopefully I will get over it? Like I so often did in the old days.'

'It's ok Charlie, you know I have forgiven you, that's the important thing, closure… and I would be lying if I said I wasn't flattered.'

'I respect you for that, but more importantly, Abi will.'

Charlotte opened her bag and brought out a white A5 white envelope and handed it tentatively to Felix. It had his name on, handwritten. It bulged a little in the middle; he was surprised she was giving him something.

'What is it?'

'You will need to sit somewhere quiet and read it, before you get home, maybe with a stiff drink. The letter will explain everything.'

'What is it Charlie?'

'The letter will explain, just trust me.'

Felix played with it in his hands, felt the texture, felt the weight of it, the hard lump in the middle. Looked down at it and then back at Charlotte.

'What is it?'

'It's a letter from me to you. No one else needs to see it, better if no one else sees it.'

'About what?'

"It would be better if you read it first, alone, without me there.' He looked back down at it and then back at her. He searched her face for clues. He looked even more confused now. ''Just read it Fe. It will explain.'

'Ok.' He agreed, reluctant. He could see she was not going to be forthcoming with its carefully premeditated contents.

'Ok Felix, this is good-bye then. I have had the most wonderful afternoon with you, I really have. It has been fantastic even with the slight you-know-what?'

She held out her arms to him, he felt uncomfortable now. She pushed a weak smile up her face. He moved towards her and she kissed him on the cheek and her voice wobbled.

'Thank you so much Fe.' Felix detected this was not a *'thank you'* for a lovely afternoon, this was something different. This felt like she was going off to do something silly, something tragic.

'What do you mean *thank you*, Charlie?'

'Thank you in advance.'

'In advance of what?'

She pulled away from him. Her gaze said: *You can go now*, his: *What are you up to Charlotte?–You've got me worried now.* She looked more serious; he was uncertain what it portrayed. He wondered if he could

117

read her like he used to able to, until... obvious he couldn't now.

'The letter will explain everything. Bye Fe.'

She turned and walked back inside. He wanted to know what riddles she was talking, but he was not chasing after her; he did not want the melodrama. He felt nauseous, uncertain whether to run after her and check on her, or just walk away: uncertain how to read the signals now. His head darted between the direction of Hyde Park and the hotel entrance. The doorman watched him, but remained quiet and discrete. Felix took a few tentative steps the few metres along the pavement and looked through the glass of the side door as she entered the lift. The attendant shut the door, *the door to the oldest working lift in London*–the abstract fact flashed into his mind. The Doorman kept his vigilance, knowing he'd just left the hotel with a resident. Felix stepped back to his original position; his head spinning; oscillating with metronomic indecision. He walked in the direction of the Park, and stopped on the corner of Brook and Davies Street, still with the hotel by his side. He knew what he had to do, even though he tried to walk away. Time seemed to slow as he stood bolt upright, tourists appearing busier passed him on both sides, his pricking internal monologue resonated, *'shit, I have to check on her, I would never forgive myself.'*

He walked back to the Hotel and entered through the side door, before the doorman could get there to open it for him. He strode through the crowd of visiting Chinese dignitaries that had not appeared to move for hours, and waited for the lift. He thought about using the stairs, just as the lift arrived. The attendant registered the worry on his face and before he could direct him, the attendant asserted.

'Floor Four Sir?'

'Yes, thanks.'

'Left something behind, Sir?'

Felix thought about the complexity of the answer and the possible scenarios awaiting him. He was so engrossed he neglected to answer him. Felix ran down the corridor to Charlotte's room and banged on the door. He could hear no foot-steps on the other side, impatient, he banged harder. The attendant had stepped from the lift and was peering down the corridor. Felix heard Charlotte's voice from within the room, '*Ok, ok, I'm coming.*'

They both seemed just as surprised to see each other. The attendant disappeared back into the lift. Charlotte noticed the envelope in his hand, but it did not look as though it had been opened, and even if it had, he would not have had time to read it all. He noticed two dresses over her arm. Felix did not know how to deal with a situation like this, so he just came straight out with it.

'You're not going to try and kill yourself are you?'

Charlotte laughed at him. Felix was not sure if it was a cleaver ploy, a deception to get rid of him.

'Is that why you came back?'

'*Yes*, I'm worried that you might do something stupid.'

His gaze alighted on the two dresses and she looked down at them and then back at him.

'No Felix.' She looked at the two dresses once more. She looked embarrassed or guilty maybe? 'I was leaving. I am going back to my own house.'

Felix was puzzled as well as being somewhat relieved, then he thought maybe she was going to do something silly there.

'I thought you were staying here tonight?'

119

'I want to go home. I'd rather go home tonight.'

'But you must have paid a fortune for the room?'

'It's only money Felix. It does not bring you happiness, believe me, I know.'

He was still perplexed; she could see it in his eyes.

'Felix, I promise you I'm not going to do anything silly. I'm through with doing stupid things.'

'How do I know you're not lying?'

She smiled a warm parental smile at him.

'I promise you Fe. Come here.' She held out her arms and moved towards him and hugged him tight. 'Thanks for coming back and checking on me–*you lovely man*.' As she pulled away she pecked him on the side of his cheek. 'Right Fe, you get off home, but not before you have read the letter I have given you.'

Felix looked down at the letter in his hand.

'Should I not read it here now?'

'No, not here, and not in the Hotel, go to a pub, or the Park, it will explain everything.'

Charlotte could see the natural bewilderment swimming in his eyes.

'It will all make sense when you read it Fe, trust me. Felix you should go now, hopefully we will meet again soon.'

'Ok, but you promise me you're not going to do anything silly. I could ring Trist?'

She smiled at him, 'As always with you Fe, *thank you*. I'm fine, you get off. No more good-byes.'

'Ok.'

Chapter 3

Felix stood outside Claridge's, equidistant between the entrance and the corner, looking at the unopened envelope with his first name on the front, playing it in his hands, feeling its weight, his fingers migrating to the protuberance in the middle, trying to guess what it could be, like he had done with Christmas presents when he was a child. He stood motionless and looked at it while people passed, while the woman from the bar earlier slipped out of the door and passed in front of him undetected. He was wondering whether he should have a quick read of it, then he could ask/challenge/confront/thank Charlotte for the words/actions/sentiments/gifts within. He realised he was dealing with too many imponderables, too many variables, and he concluded he was being ridiculous; he had to trust Charlotte, trust her and do what she had asked of him. After a moment he gripped the envelope and its contents and strode off in the direction of Hyde Park, his head still spinning; that was the effect Charlotte could have on men, on him, then and now. The activity of the metropolis was a mere backdrop now he had the envelope in his hand. It was his sole focus, he looked down at it. His mind was trying to read what was inside, guess what was enclosed. What had she put in the written word that she could not have said to him moments earlier?, especially allied with the courage offered by alcohol. Who wrote letters these days, when you had someone's e-mail address or phone number?

He was not thinking as clearly as usual, with a more lucid mind he would have known that Grosvenor Square was the nearest pleasant environment to sit and read the letter–why might he need a drink? When he stumbled across the gates at the corner of the public space, he stopped, brought the envelope up to chest level and looked past the gates, into the park and entered. The September Eleventh Memorial would be the quietest area, but an exuberant crowd of schoolchildren were swamping it. The concourse in front of the Roosevelt Statue with its eight rectangularly arranged benches would offer up a form of sanctuary somewhere, with lunchtime now well passed. A family vacated a bench under a large plane tree, and he seized the opportunity to sit down in the shade. An old man with too many clothes on for the warm weather sat on the opposite end of the bench. Felix looked at the envelope addressed to him and hesitated one last time before he unglued it with his little finger.

'Hope it is not a suicide note?'

The old man said as he laughed and Felix smiled back at him: they hoped for the same thing. A small MP3 player and earphones slipped out onto his lap and he inspected the device. The elderly man was still watching him.

"Oh, you're a spy hey. Don't worry, so am I."

He laughed as the last few words left his lips and Felix thought he smiled back.

He placed the small MP3 in a lower outside jacket pocket. He slid the letter out; it had one clean fold down the middle, unfolded it to reveal a page of typed print. He shuffled the papers to ascertain how many there were and how much reading—four A4 sides completely full. He saw his name again at the top, but no heading or date. The man stood up, he smiled and raised the palm of his hand as he drew level with Felix then shuffled away. Felix began to read:

Dearest Felix,

I know you have forgiven me for how I treated you after Oxford, or you would not have met me. Most men would have not bothered, I surmise, but that is not your nature, of all the men I have shared a bed with in my life, none compare to you, and never will.

Time can be a cruel mistress (!) and retrospect can cast a very critical eye; if only we could live our lives backwards like Benjamin Button? You never know at the time *when it is fantastic*, you think it can only stay the same or get even better; never ever worse! But when I think back now to our time together at Oxford in my room, I would have quite happily gone on having *foot-sex* with you and remained a virgin forever. God, when our bodies were one, when everything locked, when we breathed as a single organism, as soon as we ripped apart, we longed to rip back together immediately—I miss those times so much. I would give *everything* I have and be a slave forever afterwards just to have a night back in that room with us. I have asked myself a million times, why I discarded you, threw you away, and although it is easy to blame others, I can only blame myself. If you think I would not have given everything up and ran back to you after I realised I had made a stupid mistake, you are mistaken—as well as me. But I thought you would never have me back, never forgive me. Why should you? I have tortured myself, agonised over why I did it?'

I have had professional help. I am not sure if it was money well spent? If it came up in conversation, it will have been one of the three things I will have lied to you about—I am embarrassed is the answer! I deluded myself that because I am quite bright, I could heal myself—some things education never really helps with.

The other is Trist. We have always been very close and in constant contact, and a few of the others, but it is only Trist I have implored not to talk to you about me and my past (present at the time) and Margot to some extent know the whole truth, so if you want to talk to someone apart from me, Trist is the best option. Trist is the brother I never had, thankfully I never discarded him. You will have to forgive me yet again, not Trist. I always implored him not to tell you, he wanted to. He was my spy, he always kept me informed, a double agent. I thought about coming to his civil partnership, but you and Abi were there and it, I, would have caused a drunken scene and embarrassed everyone, and taken the lime-light away from David and Trist's big day. I went on honeymoon with them to Barbados and they came to New York for my wedding; that is why he was not that keen for you to holiday with them in the Caribbean! (sorry again.)

There was a moment of opportunity when you finished with Julie, when I had truly come to my senses, but it was so short, as you went from Julie to Abi so quickly; Trist put me off, or I put myself off, or both? He said you were so happy together, and I think secretly he thought you had a better chance with Abi than you did with me—and he may have been right, but he would never come out and say it. Maybe if you have divided loyalties forced upon you, the scales eventually tip one way? Whenever I come back to London, I always meet up with Trist, we go shopping, eat and get pissed, just like the good old days—Once we almost bumped into each other, we were on Oxford Road in Selfridges and you rang him, and you said you were just around the corner. You rang off and Trist said I should meet you, it would look casual, but I panicked, he said he would go with you to the Old Crown, and I should compose myself and come in, 'This has gone on too long Charlie now, you're becoming obsessive. I keep getting caught in the middle, and it is not fair on me.' I know Trist felt as unhappy as us when we separated. He could not believe it, I never told him until afterwards. He felt betrayed that he had lost his best two friends together from College and well...

When you first met Abi I hired a private detective to try and dish up some dirt on her, so I could breeze back in and take her place, cuckold my way back in. But the detective found nothing. She is a lovely woman (beautiful and funny as well—I should hate her, but it would be misplaced, and if I am totally honest, I am jealous that she makes you so happy.) Now I know that is obsessive, a bit scary, but I was fighting for you, invisible fighting, shadow boxing behind the scenes, a chink of hope was all I needed. But if I am honest, I was always torn if you would have said *yes*, you obviously wouldn't; it is now evident.

Why did I marry Steve? I married a man I liked a lot, had strong affection for, but I married him for companionship, so I would not be alone at night. It is a form of cowardice really, I know. He loved me, I did not make him, he just did, why would he not, a husband and a wife, until death do us part. How did I know I did not love him? —because I loved you, and what Steve and I had, fell too far short. I tortured myself, I should have resigned myself to a life of contentment, he gave me that, but rightly or frequently wrongly, I have been an all or nothing sort of girl. He gave me the warmth of a bonfire, but never the fireworks as well, maybe I am just greedy? Maybe I expected far too much?

I have read virtually everything you have ever written that has been published and I find it hard not to fill up most times; even when I laugh at your work, it often turns to tears—some of your theories are still flawed by the way! But I never tire of you. How could I? I have touched you, tasted you, held you, loved you, lost you

125

and never stopped loving you. It was better the first time–much better. I always told myself I would get my chance again, and even as time has slipped by very slowly. I knew that the passage of every day would leave you less bitter, and more likely to have me back, to truly forgive.

All the business I have done in the passing of time; was just filling in, trying to feel something like we had, patient waiting, like a chameleon for its prey. But now that time has obviously passed. When I read *'Love in the Time of Cholera*,' I cried for days afterwards, at the thought of waiting until we are both almost dead, or maybe more realistically, never having you back in my arms. I do not think of sex when I think of you, I think of *love*, sex is what I have with other people–incidental and transient. Love is what I have with you in my mind and in my dreams. They say it is better to have loved and lost, then never loved at all–what utter bollocks that is! Now I realise I may never get my chance again, not even a last waltz, I have to ask you something. It will sound crazy and you will have to think about it for a while, I appreciate that, I only ask you now because I am desperate, in more ways than one.

It will have come up in conversation, I will have engineered it. I want to have a baby, more importantly your baby or babies. My mother went through the menopause at forty and so did my Gran, so the biological clock is ticking louder and louder. There are a number of ways of doing this, the preferred one for me, and by far the most enjoyable, may not be an option, but it only need be the once, but I can tell you now, I will *cry, no*, sob uncontrollably afterwards, having fleetingly tasted it again, but they would be tears of joy as well as sadness; I would be nineteen again, *still* a teenager and be transported to a better place.

The next easiest option is if you leave a sample at Trist's and I pop round with the turkey baster! I could pretend to be a lesbian if it helps!! You need not see me; he can put it in the fridge. (It would be funny if it were not so sad?)

Another option is you make an anonymous donation at a sperm clinic and I pay them for your sperm. This way you can almost legitimately say you knew nothing about it.

This is not just a random day that we have met, this the middle of my cycle, my most fertile. If it had all gone to plan, the deal would have been the same. In all honesty I may not have told you before hand, if that had been the case I may not have informed you about the baby at all—I do not know, is the honest truth.

I appreciate what I am asking you is momentous and life changing – for me anyway. I would understand why you would say no, you owe me very little or maybe nothing for how I treated you, but I will point out, unfairly, I know: Think of all the good times together, née fantastic times we had together. I ask you as a monument to that, to the best two years of my life, with the best man I have ever met, the only man I can compare with my own dad.

The next logical question is provision for the baby (sorry, sounds a bit Victorian), but you need to know as (hopefully) the biological father of my child.

I will look after it myself and employ a full time nanny. It will want for nothing, I would strive hard to make sure it was grounded and level-headed—I know you would detest a spoilt child. Hopefully I have proven to you that I am now capable of bringing a child up (if I have not done myself justice, and you have a hideous image of Miss Havisham, I probably drank too much,

127

out of sheer nervousness. I may have hidden it well–I've had a lot of practice).

I will live south of the river in a house with a garden, so there is no chance that we could accidentally bang into each other… *although −sorry!* (I will live outside London if you prefer?)

I will never tell a living soul that you are the biological father. Trist will pretend to be, so that covers a few bases. I give you my word, and having read this and meeting me, you will know my word is my bond.

There are obviously other options available, if you so desire, but I must stress that Trist will always claim to be the biological father. He says it might draw to a close this *charade;* that is not what I call it, for me it is more than a melodrama.

You could visit your child whenever you wanted, I need not be there, Trist will or the Nanny will be the go between. I know it is mad, but it is an option.

You may just want to see the baby after it is born, or never at all. But I do hope at some point, maybe in the future, the brothers and sisters meet each other and have a chance to talk about their wonderful father together–it's a long way off, and maybe I always hope for far too much?

I know what I am asking you sounds crazy, almost bordering on the insane, but I don't want sperm from a man I don't know, a man I know nothing about, care nothing for. I know if it is half of you, I can love the baby even more. I would love it anyway, but if it was half you, I would have the contentment of knowing it would turn out to be a fine human being. Every time I hugged it or looked at it, it would remind me of our time at Lady Margaret's and I would smile and know it was not a complete waste letting you go.

What we had; the majesty of it; may have long been dampened for you, but for me, well you know by now...

If I could turn back the clock, if I could slide open the doors back to that room, I would sell my soul to the devil, the sad thing is I used to blame my mother for everything, but after this long being a grown-up, I don't think I can use that get out clause anymore? I cannot blame anyone but myself, and that's the thing that makes me the saddest of all, *the beast that stalks me*.

Please do me this one *gigantic* favour, far beyond the call of any duty–I probably don't deserve it, and now is the time for revenge if you so desire – but I *implore you* as a friend, and a testament to what we once had. I tried to find more words, clever words, a poem that said it all, and then I heard an Adele song on the radio –*Someone Like You*, (it's on the MP3 player) and it said more than a poem, because you felt her pain, the emotion of her loss as she sang it. If you say no, I truly understand, I will not think any worse of you, but I had to ask... *for me, it isn't over.*

Love,
Charlotte.
Xx

He did not need to put the MP3 player on; he knew the song already–it was one of Abi's favourites. Felix re-read the letter–slower this time, folded it and put it back in the envelope, stood up and started to walk down the path towards the entrance–the same entrance he had come through. Not the quickest way home–he was not thinking straight.

The End…

Other books by Ian M Pindar:

Hoofing It - First in the Robert Knight Series

In 1996, just before university, Robert and his best friend Spud hedonistically set off around Europe in their neighbour's ~~borrowed~~ stolen car, with the £28,000 they have 'acquired,' forged documents, no insurance and class A's under the bonnet. On the way to the ferry in Hull, they save the life of a young suicidal woman, Naomi, who is about to jump off the Humber Bridge. All her immediate family have tragically died in a car crash one year previous. Robert is adamant he can help rehabilitate her; but Steven wants nothing of this 'Captain Freedom' talk. Along the way they meet a beautiful smack-head – dance like the rest of the world is watching – reach a higher state of consciousness - have gratuitous sex – perpetrate sweet criminal acts – meet madness and genius in equal measure – open the door to hell – have perfect moments – cry in the Vatican – have scary liaisons – get mortally challenged – blow things up and see hope boil away.

i

Hoofed - Second in the Robert Knight Series

Tazmin and Rob's love has endured and grown throughout their time at university, even though they were separated by two hundred miles. Tazmin believes that by finishing with him on the eve of his around the world trip, she is setting him free to have a better time travelling - unhindered. It is not what he wants, but he has no choice in the matter; he only wants Tazmin to be with him, but she will not leave her new job in the theatre. Will their love survive the trials and tribulations of the year; the near death experiences, drugs, arrests and sexual misdemeanours; or will fate and distance conspire against them? Only time - which waits for no man, will tell.

The final instalment of the Robert Knight series: *The Space Between the Notes* will be out in 2015.

50 Mistakes of the Fledgling Fiction Writer
(Non-fiction)

'50 Mistakes of the Fledgling Fiction Writer' is a brief guide (30,000 words) to the most common mistakes that the novice can make, or does not even consider when trying or thinking about writing their first novel. A lot of authors have gone to the effort of sharing their 'craft', but not many can think back to the very start of the writing journey and all the extras that entails. Ian M Pindar can, that is why he has produced this book. By the end you will know whether the psychological, emotion and time-consuming toil will be worth the effort!

iv

Made in the USA
Charleston, SC
20 December 2014